THE HOLY WAR

THELMA H. JENKINS

JOHN BUNYAN'S: THE HOLY WAR

Foreword by

Dr D. Martyn Lloyd-Jones

EVANGELICAL PRESS

P.O. Box 5, Welwyn, Herts. AL6 9NU
P.O. Box 2453, Grand Rapids, Mich. 49501, U.S.A.

The Holy War: John Bunyan
First published in 1682

A Version for To-day: Thelma H. Jenkins
First edition: Evangelical Press 1976

ISBN 0 85234 074 5

Illustrations by LEWIS F. LUPTON
Cover design by PETER WAGSTAFF

Printed in Great Britain by Stanley L. Hunt (Printers) Ltd,
Rushden, Northamptonshire

Contents

Foreword

Nothing, perhaps, provides us with a better index to the quality of life of an individual or a generation of Christian people, than their reading habits.

Many, alas, do not seem to read at all, but just spend their time in talking or arguing, or in attending an endless succession of meetings. Others read nothing but exciting and dramatised accounts of other people's experiences. Still others are interested only in books and booklets which deal with "the Christian attitude" to this, that and the other.

Most significant of all, however, is our attitude to the great classics of the Christian life, the books in which our forefathers delighted, and on which, next to the Bible itself, they fed their souls. In this category the works of John Bunyan always stood out prominently for some 250 years, and their neglect during the past 50 years exposes the pathetic superficiality of our generation.

It is said that the moderns find Bunyan difficult to read. Because of this, Mrs. Thelma Jenkins, in her desire to introduce people to the riches of "The Holy War" in particular, has undertaken this labour of love. Her desire is, that as a result of reading it in this more modern idiom, many may be led to read Bunyan himself directly, and thereby experience untold blessings and great enrichment of their spiritual lives.

It is my pleasure to encourage this noble effort and my privilege to pray that God will bless it to that end.

D. M. Lloyd-Jones.

Preface

"This allegory is believed by very many to be the most beautiful and extraordinary that mere human genius ever composed in any language."

So wrote George Offor over a century ago, concerning "The Holy War". Had I read those words before re-writing this book, I am certain that I would never have had the temerity to attempt such a thing; yet it was its rich spiritual depth that was truly my incentive.

In these days, when there are so many vulgar and blasphemous caricatures abroad concerning the Lord Jesus Christ, I long that God might be pleased to use this book to reveal the surpassing majesty, dignity and beauty of His Son, Emmanuel. For many years it has been my frequent prayer that I might "serve my generation according to the counsel and purpose of God" (Acts 13:36). If, through the reading of this easier version of Bunyan's allegory, some may be led to see, as they have never seen before, the loveliness of Emmanuel and the marvel of God's pardoning grace to the utterly undeserving, I shall dare to hope that part of that prayer has been answered.

THELMA H. JENKINS.

Introduction

Mansoul

THE CITY OF MANSOUL

This city is, of course, Man's Soul, which at the first God made holy and innocent. Bunyan's allegory shows, in word pictures, how man lost his first position of innocence by listening to the temptations of Satan, how he came under Satan's domination and the misery that followed, and how the Lord Jesus Christ came to rescue man from his bondage to Satan, casting out the evil within him and making his heart fit once more to be the dwelling-place of God. The story also illustrates the evil consequences and misery of turning from the Lord and the tenderness of God in restoring the penitent backslider.

List of Characters

It may be that some who are new to the Christian faith will not easily recognise all the meaning hidden within this allegory. For this reason, a list of the main characters is given below for quick and easy reference whilst reading the story.

The Great King, El Shaddai	God the Father.
The Golden Prince, Emmanuel	God the Son.
The Lord Secretary	God the Holy Spirit.
The Captains Boanerges, Judgement, Conviction and Execution	The Law of God.
The Captains Faith, Good-hope, Love, Purity and Patience	The Gospel of God and the blessings and graces which accompany Emmanuel.
The Townsmen of Mansoul	The thoughts, emotions and feelings within man's soul.
Diabolus, the usurping prince and tyrant	The Devil.
Lucifer, Beelzebub, Legion, Apollyon	Various names used in the Scriptures to describe the Devil.
The Diabolonians	The evil, sinful thoughts, emotions and feelings within man's soul after the Fall.

Other characters will easily be understood by their actual names.

PART ONE

DOWNFALL AND REDEMPTION

Chapter One

Mansoul Listens to the Tempter

There was once a fair and beautiful city called Mansoul. This city had been built by the great king El Shaddai for his own pleasure and delight and, of all the things made by this wise and good king, Mansoul was undoubtedly the masterpiece.

In the midst of the city was a famous and stately palace,[1] strong as a castle, yet beautiful enough to be the residence of so great a king. It had been built for this very purpose – that El Shaddai himself might dwell there and rule, alone,

[1] The heart.

in wisdom and love. The wall of the town was exceedingly strong, being built in such a way that no enemy from outside could break in, and no harm could come to the city, except by consent of the townsmen within. Five gates were set in the walls, for entering or leaving the city and these, again, could never be opened by force from outside, but only by the willingness of those inside. The names of the gates were – Ear Gate, Eye Gate, Mouth Gate, Nose Gate and Feel Gate.

When Mansoul was first built by El Shaddai it was in perfect condition. There was provision of everything needful stored within its walls and it had the most excellent law that has ever been formed. There was not one deceitful person within its gates; all its men were true men, all loyal to each other, which was no small blessing. Over and above all this, Mansoul enjoyed the protection, favour and delight of the king's own presence (for so long as it remained true to him).

Now I must tell you that a great enemy arose against Mansoul: a mighty giant, who determined that he would overthrow the great king and have this fair city for his own dwelling. Who was this enemy? The Scriptures call him Satan, or Diabolus. At one time, he had been a high-ranking servant of King El Shaddai, enjoying much honour and glory in his position. Sadly, however, his heart was lifted up in pride within him, so that he coveted the position of being next to El Shaddai himself, a dignity and honour that already belonged to the king's beloved son, Emmanuel. Well, Diabolus plotted with a few of his ambitious companions and they agreed together to revolt against their king and seize the coveted position. How foolish they were, for the king and his son, possessing all knowledge, could not but know of their treason. Diabolus and his companions were convicted of this horrible conspiracy and not only were they cast out of their previous positions of honour and rank, they were also banished eternally from the courts of the king, never to expect any favour from him again.

Realising that they had forever forfeited their honour and the favour of their king, what did these miserable creatures do but add to their former pride a terrible rage and malice against both El Shaddai and his son. As they roved from place to place, burning to find something of the king's upon which they might revenge themselves, they came at length to the city of Mansoul. Knowing that El Shaddai had built and beautified this place for himself, they were filled with horrible joy at the thought of making an assault upon, and perhaps of taking, the very delight of the king for their own possession.

"Now," they said, "we have found how to be revenged upon the king. Let us take counsel together, and see how we may best accomplish the capture of this city." They forthwith held a council of war and set themselves to answer these four questions. Shall we *all* show ourselves to the town of Mansoul, or send a representative? Shall we let them see us in our present ragged and beggarly condition? Shall we tell Mansoul plainly what we are after, or approach them with trickery and deceit? Shall we endeavour to shoot one of the principal men of the city; that is, the one who may cause us the most difficulty?

"In answer to the first question," said Diabolus, "I say no, we must not all show ourselves, lest we put the townspeople in a fright – because if they take alarm, we shall never win the town, since no-one can enter without their consent. Let a few, or even one, be sent to assault Mansoul and let *me* be that one."

The council all agreed to this and came to their next question. After some discussion, Beelzebub advised that Diabolus should definitely go in disguise – but *what* disguise?

"Why not go disguised as an animal?" suggested Lucifer. "You could take the form of one of those animals over which they have dominion? They would be less likely to suspect such a one of making an assault upon them."

This suggestion was received with applause and it was finally decided that Diabolus should take the form of a dragon, which was a familiar enough sight in those days.

After another lengthy discussion they resolved not to state plainly their intentions because, as we have already remarked, the inhabitants of Mansoul were a strong people in a strong town, who could not be won without their own consent.

"Besides which," added Legion, "if they realise what we are up to, they will immediately cry to their king for help and that will quickly be the end of us. Let us rather approach them with flattering words, lies and promises, pretending things that will never happen and promising them things which they will never receive. This will be the way to win them, inducing them to open their gates of their own accord, for they are an innocent people, quite unused to lying, deceit and hypocrisy. They will, therefore, believe everything we say, imagining it all to be true, especially if we pretend great love for them and great concern for their honour and advantage."

It was felt that this crafty counsel could not be bettered and all that remained to be decided was whether to shoot one of the principal townsmen and, if so, which one? Everyone agreed that this would be a wise course to take and it was decided, if at all possible, to destroy Captain Resistance, for he was a great man in Mansoul, and the one whom Diabolus and his company feared more than any other. So, the council of war having ended, this evil band then marched against Mansoul, all of them being invisible except Diabolus, who was disguised as a dragon.

Drawing near to the city, they all sat down near Ear Gate while Diabolus sounded his trumpet to call for audience. Upon hearing this, the chief men of the town of Mansoul came to the wall to see what was the matter. There were Lord Innocent, Lord Willbewill, Lord Understanding (the Lord Mayor), Mr. Conscience (the Recorder) and Captain Resistance. Lord Willbewill was their spokesman and he demanded to know why the town had been roused in this unusual manner. Meek as a lamb, Diabolus answered, and a very fine speech he made.

"Gentlemen of the famous town of Mansoul! As you can see, I am one who is bound by your king to do you homage and service and this is my very reason for approaching you. I have come to seek *your* advantage, not my own, and to tell you how you may be delivered from the bondage in which you are held, although you are at present unaware of it."

At this, the men of Mansoul pricked up their ears.

"Bondage?" they said. "Of what bondage does he speak?"

Thus, having their attention and curiosity from the start, Diabolus proceeded.

"I have something to say to you about your king and his laws and how they affect yourselves. I know, of course, that your king is both great and powerful; yet all that he has told you is not true. He has said that if you do so small a thing as to eat the fruit that he has forbidden, you will die. Now that is *not* true; you will *not* surely die! Even worse than that, the very thing he forbids you to do is something that would be of most benefit to you. The tree that he has forbidden you to touch is called 'the tree of the knowledge of good and evil', and you cannot imagine how pleasant its fruit is, or how much to be desired it is, while you obey your king's commandment. You are kept in blindness and ignorance, yet you pride yourselves that you are a free people. You are not free; you are held down and deprived and that for the sole reason that your king will have it so. Why, how grievous it is, that you should be kept back from the very thing that would most benefit you, giving you both wisdom and honour, so that your eyes would be opened and you would be like gods!"

At this point, while Diabolus was still speaking, one of the invisible company shot at Captain Resistance, mortally wounding him in the head so that, to the amazement of the townspeople and the secret delight of Diabolus, he fell over the wall, dead. Now, he being the only man of war in Mansoul, the people had no more heart to resist, which was just as Diabolus would have it. Then stood forth the one whom he had brought as his spokesman and, making himself now visible to the townsmen, he began to address them as follows:

"Gentlemen, it makes my master and myself happy to see you all listening so quietly and attentively, for we hope between us to give you good advice. You must realise that my master has such great love for you that he is prepared to speak to you for your good, even though he risks the severe anger of the great El Shaddai by so doing. There is, I am sure, little need for me to add to his words. Why, the very name of the tree, 'the knowledge of good and evil', will surely convince you. I therefore only add this word, with his gracious permission" (this with an oily smile and a most servile bow towards Diabolus). "Consider his words; look at the tree and look at its promising fruit. Remember also, that as yet you know very little, and to eat of the fruit of *this* tree will give you greatly increased knowledge."

Now when the townspeople saw that the fruit of the tree was good to eat, most pleasant to the eyes and, above all, a tree that could make them wiser than they then were, they followed this evil advice and picked and ate of its fruit. I forgot to tell you that, as this crafty orator was speaking,

Lord Innocent staggered and fell down where he stood, and no efforts could bring him to life again. So both Captain Resistance and Lord Innocent died, these two brave men, who were the finest and noblest in the whole city of Mansoul and, there being none others so noble, all the remaining townspeople yielded obedience to Diabolus and became his slaves, as you will hear. For, upon eating the forbidden fruit, they forgot all about their good king El Shaddai and his law and the solemn warning he had given them. They forthwith opened both Ear Gate and Eye Gate and in swarmed Diabolus with his now visible followers.

Chapter Two

Diabolus, the Tyrant Prince

Having made such an easy entrance through the gates, Diabolus proceeded to march right through the centre of the town in the direction of Heart Castle. Finding all the people very warmly inclined towards him, he decided to strike while the iron was hot and, pausing in the midst of his triumphal march, he made a further speech.

"Alas, my dear Mansoul," he said, "although I have done you this service in promoting you to honour and greatly increasing your liberty, I see that you are much in need of one who will protect and defend you. I fear that when El

Shaddai hears of this, he will come quickly, for he will be grieved that you have managed at last to throw off his bonds and laws. What will you do? Will you let him again enslave you?"

Then these foolish, bewitched people all cried out, "We want *you* to reign over us", which, of course, was just what the cunning Diabolus was hoping they would say. Without delay, he agreed to become their prince and, taking possession of Heart Castle, he promptly strengthened it with all manner of things against El Shaddai, or any other, who might try to regain the town to his obedience. So this beautiful castle, built in Mansoul by El Shaddai for his own delight and pleasure, now became a den and stronghold for the evil giant Diabolus. Having done this much, Diabolus was still not satisfied that all was secure, so he began to remodel the town, promoting some and putting down others. He began with the Lord Mayor (who was otherwise called Lord Understanding) and Mr. Conscience, the Recorder.

Although Lord Understanding had been amongst those who had willingly agreed to admit him to the city, Diabolus thought it safer to remove him from his high office. (Diabolus was rather afraid of him, knowing that he still had a fair understanding of many things.) He therefore not only took away his leading position, but craftily built a high tower that would stand between the sun's reflection and the windows of Lord Understanding's palace, so that he lived in continual darkness and, being kept from the light, he became as one who had been born blind. Not only so, but he was kept a prisoner within his own palace and grounds and, even had he the desire to help Mansoul, what could he have done for it? This was the sad condition of Lord Understanding all the time that Diabolus ruled over the town.

As for Mr. Conscience, before the town was overrun by Diabolus, he had been a man very well read in the laws of his king, one who was both bold and brave to speak the truth on every occasion. Now Diabolus could not bear Mr. Conscience for, with all his tricks and wiles, he could not get him under his control. Although Mr. Conscience had largely turned away from his true king, being well-pleased with much of the tyrant's laws and service, yet, every now and then, he would remember some of the king's laws, and speak out with such a terrible and powerful voice that he not only made the whole town of Mansoul shake and tremble, but even caused Diabolus to feel afraid of him.

Since Diabolus could not wholly control Mr. Conscience, he led him, little by little, into many wicked ways, until he had managed to make the old man's mind both hard and stupid; so much so, that he had almost no conscience about sin at all. Being unable to progress any further in that direction, Diabolus thought of another idea, which was to persuade the men of the town that Mr. Conscience was mad and, therefore, not to be listened to.

"For," said Diabolus, "if he is not mad, why does he sometimes rant and rave against things that are done, and at other times say nothing at all? These are just the fits of a madman."

So, in one way or another, Diabolus quickly caused Mansoul utterly to disregard and despise anything said by Mr. Conscience. He also had a way of making the old man merry at times, so that he would deny the very things that he had said so firmly a little while before, or alternatively, support things which a while before he had condemned. He never now spoke willingly for El Shaddai, but seemed often to be fast asleep, or even dead, so that he was really no use to Mansoul at all.

Sparing no efforts, Diabolus would sometimes say, "O

Mansoul, in spite of the ravings of Mr. Conscience and the clamour of his thunderous words, you notice that you hear nothing of King Shaddai himself". (This, I would have you know, was a barefaced lie, for every outcry of Mr. Conscience against the sin of Mansoul was really the voice of their true king speaking to them.) "You can see," the tyrant would add, "that your king sets very little value upon you, for he has made no attempt to deliver you, or to call you to account for what you have done. He knows," he said, with a wily grin, "that though you were once his, now you are mine, and he has given us over to each other for ever.

"Moreover, O Mansoul," he would continue, "consider how greatly I have served you. I do not doubt that my new laws and customs give you greater happiness and contentment than you ever knew before. I have given you greater liberty and freedom and, whereas I found you much restricted, *I* have not laid any laws or rules upon you. You each live as a prince, ruling your own life, and I call none of you to account – except the madman" (meaning Mr. Conscience).

Thus would Diabolus quieten the town whenever Mr. Conscience should burst forth (as he occasionally did), or he would rouse the townsmen to such fury against the old man (they so hated the very sight or remembrance of him) that they would wish that he were dead, or a thousand miles away from them. But for all their fury, somehow, no doubt by the wisdom of El Shaddai, Mr. Conscience was yet preserved within the city of Mansoul. His house, fortunately, was as strong as a castle and if ever the townsmen came in a mob seeking to destroy him, he would open the sluice gates, letting out floods that would drown them if they did not hasten away.[1]

[1] Fears of judgement.

Let us leave Mr. Conscience, however, and see how another of the gentry of the town fared, namely, Lord Willbewill. Now this man was very high-born and more of a free-holder than any. He was a man of great strength, courage and resolution, but, whether because of pride in his position or his privileges (but certainly through pride of some kind), he quite refused to become a slave in Mansoul but determined that he would serve Diabolus by gaining some governing position under him. This he did quite easily, for he had been one of the first to accept the counsel of Diabolus when he held forth at Ear Gate and to agree to open the gate, so that Diabolus was kindly inclined toward him from the beginning and, seeing the strength and courage of the man, was only too pleased to have him as one of his principal officers. The giant, therefore, had a heart-to-heart talk with him, but Willbewill needed little persuasion, being quite willing to serve the tyrant, as long as he could obtain a leading position. He was therefore appointed the Captain of the Castle,[1] Governor of the Wall[2] and Keeper of the Gates[3] in the town of Mansoul. A clause was even added to his commission that nothing should henceforth be done without his will and pleasure in all the town of Mansoul. In this way Lord Willbewill became the very next in rank to Diabolus himself. His clerk was a man called Mr. Mind, who followed his master implicitly, always speaking and doing exactly as he indicated.[4]

Now that power had been put into his hand, Willbewill at once showed himself for the man he was. First, he flatly denied that he owed any loyalty to his former lord and king, El Shaddai. This done, he took an oath, swearing fidelity to his great master Diabolus and then set to work on the town itself. He spoke evil of Mr. Conscience at every

[1] The heart. [2] The flesh. [3] The senses.

[4] In this way Mansoul was made to fulfil the evil desires of the flesh and of the mind.

opportunity and could not endure either to see or hear him, shutting his eyes and stopping his ears if ever he met him or heard him speak. Neither could he bear that even a fragment of El Shaddai's law should be seen anywhere in the town. Mr. Mind, his clerk, had in his possession a few old, torn parchments of the good laws of King Shaddai, but Lord Willbewill would not so much as look at them but cast them behind his back. (It is true that Mr. Conscience also had a few of these laws in his study, but Lord Willbewill could not lay his hands on these.) He even complained if Lord Understanding had so much as a candle in his windows.[1] Nothing now pleased Willbewill but what pleased his Lord Diabolus and he would trumpet about the streets the brave nature, the wise conduct and the glory of his new prince. He would even mingle in the streets amongst the basest fellows,[2] acting with them in all manner of evil and mischievous doings.

Once the giant Diabolus had made his position secure, he set about defacing certain parts of the town. In the market place of Mansoul, and also upon the gate of the castle, was a splendid image of El Shaddai, engraved in purest gold. This image was such an exact resemblance of the great king that there was not another like it in the whole world. This was not only defaced (at the order of the tyrant and by the hand of Mr. No-Truth) but in its place was set up the horrible and fearful image of Diabolus, thus showing the town's contempt for its former king. In addition, Lord Willbewill aiding him, Mr. No-Truth was also ordered to seek out and destroy, by burning, every law-book, or book of instructions containing the commands of the king, so that not a trace of the good rule of El Shaddai might remain. Instead of these, Diabolus set up, in all public

[1] An evil will loves a darkened understanding.
[2] Vain thoughts.

places, his own vain orders and commandments, which gave liberty to the lusts of the flesh, the lusts of the eyes and the pride of life. He greatly encouraged evil and immoral behaviour and all forms of ungodliness and wickedness, promising the townspeople peace, joy and contentment in following his evil commands, assuring them that they would never be called to give an account of their actions.

Having completely disabled the Lord Mayor (Lord Understanding) and Mr. Conscience, Diabolus did not wish the people of Mansoul to charge him with having lowered their dignity, so he appointed for them a new Lord Mayor and a new Recorder, men of his own choosing. The new Lord Mayor was one called Lord Evil-Desire, a man who acted always and entirely according to his low, beastly nature. The new Recorder was one called Forget-Good, a wretched fellow indeed, who could remember nothing but evil and delighted in all that was mischievous and hurtful. These two, Lord Evil-Desire and Mr. Forget-Good, working together, by their example and encouragement successfully turned the common people into evil ways, for it is a well known fact that when those who are in a high position smile at evil, the whole region and country around them are quickly corrupted. New aldermen were appointed, from whom magistrates and councillors might be selected, and a sorry group they were, as you will see from some of their names: Unbelief, Haughty, Swearing, Hard-Heart, Fury, No-Truth, Cheating, Quick-to-Lie, Drunkenness and Atheism (Unbelief being the eldest and Atheism the youngest of the company).

Now, at last, Diabolus thought himself safe indeed. He had captured Mansoul and made his garrison strong; he had put down all the old officers and appointed new ones of his own choosing; he had defaced the image of El Shaddai, setting up his own instead; he had destroyed the ancient law-books and substituted his own sets of lies; he had set up new aldermen and magistrates, men after his own heart and he had built new strongholds which were governed by men of evil purpose.

All this he did in case the good King Shaddai, or his son, should ever come and seek to regain the city of Mansoul.

Chapter Three

The Diabolical Armour

Now you will surely think that, by this time, word must have reached the court of the good King Shaddai, informing him that Mansoul had been overrun by the giant Diabolus, his one-time servant. A messenger truly brought the sad news to the king, relating in detail how, first, Captain Resistance had been slain, then Lord Innocent had fallen down dead, killed with grief at hearing his great king so abused by a foul Diabolonian, and that the simple towns-people, believing the lies so cunningly set before them, had opened Ear Gate, letting in Diabolus and all his evil followers. The messenger then told of all that had befallen Lord Understanding and Mr. Conscience, and how Lord Willbewill was now heart and soul in the service of the tyrant, with Mr. Mind as his clerk, and that these two were ruling the town and leading the common people into all manner of wickedness.

"Indeed," added the messenger, "Lord Willbewill has openly turned against his king, giving his faith and entire loyalty to Diabolus. As if all this were not enough, the new tyrant of Mansoul (once a famous but now perishing town) has set up a new Lord Mayor and a new Recorder of his own choice, two of the vilest men in the town, namely, Lord Evil-Desire and Mr. Forget-Good." He also told of the new strongholds, finally describing how the people were now all armed in case El Shaddai should come and endeavour to reduce them to their former obedience.

This news was not delivered privately, but in open court before the king, his son, and all the high lords, chief captains and nobles. It was amazing to see the grief and distress that was caused by these evil tidings of the fall of Mansoul. Only the king and his son showed no surprise, having foreseen this years before and having even taken steps, unknown to anyone else, to provide for the relief of the town. Nevertheless, both the king and his son were deeply grieved to hear of the misery of Mansoul, showing what love and compassion they felt for this fallen and suffering town.

When the king and his son had retired, they again privately consulted together about their plans, laid long ago, concerning the recovery of Mansoul, which was to take place in such a way that the king and his son would receive eternal fame and glory thereby. The son of El Shaddai was a noble and beautiful person, who always had great affection and pity for those who were in distress (but who also bore a mortal enmity in his heart against Diabolus who, you recall, had once schemed to take his crown and his royal dignity). This son, after their consultation, entered into an agreement with his father that he would be his servant for the recovery of Mansoul, vowing that nothing should ever make him swerve from this purpose. It was designed that at a certain time, predetermined by both of them, the king's son should take a journey into the world and there, in justice and equity, make amends for the follies and sins of Mansoul, in this way laying a foundation for the perfect deliverance of the town from the tyranny of Diabolus. Emmanuel – for that was the name of this princely one – also resolved to make war against Diabolus while he was still in possession of Mansoul, drive him out of his nest and take the town to himself for his own habitation.

An order was now given to the Lord Chief Secretary to draw up a record of all that had been determined[1] and to cause it to be published in all the corners of the Kingdom of the World. Let me here give you a short summary of the contents:

> "Let all men know that Emmanuel, the son of El Shaddai the great king, has undertaken, in covenant with his father, to recover Mansoul, and not only so but, by the power of his incomparable love, to put Mansoul into an even better and happier condition than it was in before it was captured by Diabolus."

These papers were published, therefore, in several places, much to the annoyance of Diabolus who feared that he was now to be disturbed in his comfortable enjoyment of Mansoul.

I should have told you that when this great purpose of King Shaddai and his son was first made known in the heavenly court, there was a great stir amongst the high lords, nobles and captains. First it was whispered, then it

[1] The Holy Scripture.

began to ring through the king's palace, as they all wondered and marvelled at this glorious design which had been planned for the saving of the miserable Mansoul. They were not content even to keep the news in the court but some of them came down and told it in the World.

This was how the news first came to the ears of Diabolus, who was naturally very disturbed and angry to think that such things were being designed against him. After some thought, he decided to take a few precautionary measures.

Firstly, if possible, he would prevent these good tidings from ever reaching the ears of the people in Mansoul.

"For," he reasoned with himself, "if they once know that El Shaddai, their former king, and Emmanuel his son are working for the good of the town, they may well revolt against me." With renewed flattery, therefore, he strictly charged Lord Willbewill to keep watch, by day and by night, at all the gates of the town, especially Ear Gate and Eye Gate.

"My reason for this," he informed his henchman, "is that I have heard that there is a design afoot to make us all traitors and to reduce Mansoul to its former state of bondage. I hope these are only rumours, but I am sure they are as unwelcome to you as they are to me. You, therefore, must nip in the bud any such tales which may come to the people, ensuring that a strong guard is kept daily at every gate. Let no-one be admitted unless, upon examination, they plainly favour our excellent government. Let there be spies mingling with the people, with power to suppress and destroy any who speak of El Shaddai and his plans, or who appear to be plotting against us." Lord Willbewill listened carefully to his master and very diligently obeyed his commands in every respect.

Secondly, Diabolus drew up a new and horrible covenant with the people, namely, that they would never desert their prince Diabolus or his government, nor betray him, nor seek to alter his laws; but would acknowledge and own him as their rightful prince in defiance of any who might come pretending to lay claim to the town of Mansoul.

He thought, by this, to bind the people to himself in such a way that El Shaddai could never set them free. Foolish, stupid Mansoul made no demur at all, but swallowed the whole thing without any argument as easily as a whale might swallow a sprat! So far from being troubled by this new and evil covenant, they bragged and boasted of their faithfulness to their tyrant prince, vowing openly that they would *never* turn from him, or forsake him for another.

In case even these precautions should be insufficient, Diabolus, in his insane jealousy, tried to turn the town to yet more evil ways. To this end he caused a most disreputable and vile notice to be drawn up by Mr. Filth and nailed up on the castle gate, giving licence to all his trusty followers in Mansoul to indulge in every manner of filthy and loathsome conduct that appealed to them. No man was to hinder them in any way, on pain of incurring the severe displeasure of their prince. He hoped, by doing this, to make the town weaker and weaker so that, if news of deliverance should come to them, they might not put any hope in it, concluding that they were now *so* sinful that no deliverance could be possible.[1] Also, if Emmanuel knew how utterly foul the townspeople now were, how thoroughly given over to lust and vice, he might change his mind about delivering them. Diabolus knew, from his own bitter experience, that El Shaddai and Emmanuel were exceedingly holy and, perhaps, in view of its increased vileness, they would cast off Mansoul for ever.

Thirdly, he decided to forestall any news that might seep

[1] For reason says, the greater the sinner, the less grounds to hope for mercy.

through, by convincing the town that El Shaddai was sending an army intending to destroy rather than to deliver them. He accordingly summoned all the people together to the market-place where, with his usual craft and deceit, he began to address them:

"Gentlemen, and my very good friends! You are all, as you know, my legal subjects, and you are well aware how I have behaved myself amongst you from the first day that I was with you until now, and what liberty and great privileges you have enjoyed under my government. Now, my famous Mansoul, I am sorry indeed to tell you that news has come of trouble abroad – trouble that may well affect our town. I have received a message from Lord Lucifer that your former king, El Shaddai, is raising an army to come against you intending to destroy you, root and branch. For this reason, I have called you together to advise you what may be done. I could easily take care of myself, did I only consider my personal wellbeing, but my heart is so firmly united to you that I am unwilling to leave you in this danger. I am willing, rather, to stand by and fight with you to the very end. What do you say, O Mansoul? Will you desert your friend, or shall we stand together?"

As one man, the townspeople shouted out their allegiance to Diabolus, crying, "Let him who thinks otherwise be put to death!"

"Well then," continued the lying Diabolus, "it is useless for us to hope for mercy, for this King Shaddai does not know how to show it. True, to begin with, he may talk of mercy or pretend it, but only so that he may gain the mastery of the town more easily. Whatever he says, therefore, believe not a word of it, for it will all prove to be a trick to overcome us and then he will destroy us all, without mercy! I suggest that we resist him to the last man, refusing to listen to him on any terms, for therein will lie our greatest danger. I hope you know better than to allow yourselves to be ruined by flattering speeches.

"Let me make a further point," he added. "Just suppose he should make us yield and saved some of our lives, some of the underlings, what do you suppose would happen to those of you whom I have set in positions of authority, by reason of your faithfulness to me? Suppose he actually refrained from killing you, it would only be for the purpose of holding you in a worse bondage than you ever knew before and then what use would your lives be to you? Do not think for one moment that you would be allowed to live in the pleasure you have at present while I am your prince. No, you would be bound by laws that pinch and made to do things that you hate and detest.

"I say, therefore, that it is better to fight and to die fighting, than to live like slaves; and I don't mind adding that even the life of a slave would be thought too good for Mansoul now. Every blast of El Shaddai's trumpet cries out for the blood of Mansoul. Be advised by me then. Arm yourselves for battle while there is yet time and let me teach you some of the arts of war. I have plenty of armour, sufficient to arm you from top to toe. Come to my castle and let me fit you with all that you will need."

Hereupon, all the townsmen trooped after Diabolus to his castle, where they were issued with his diabolical armour.

"Here is my *helmet*, called vain hope, the hope that all will be well at the end, whatever life we have lived: a fine piece of armour this, which has been greatly used by all who expected to have peace although they had walked in wickedness. This will ward off many a blow, my Mansoul.

"Next, there is my *breastplate*, made of iron, with which all my soldiers are armed. In plain language it is called a hard heart, a heart as hard as iron, with no more feeling than a stone. If you can keep this, neither mercy will win you, nor threatenings of judgement frighten you. A hard heart is a piece of armour most necessary for all who hate El Shaddai and who would fight against him under my banner.

"My *sword* is an evil tongue, one that has been set on fire by hell and can adapt itself to speak all manner of evil against El Shaddai, his son, his ways and his people. I advise you to use this constantly. It has been tried thousands of times and whoever uses it as I instruct will never be conquered by my enemy.

"Here is my *shield* which is called unbelief, that is, questioning the truth of the word that El Shaddai has spoken, in particular, all he has said concerning the judgement of wicked men. Those who have written about the wars between Emmanuel and my servants have always testified that he could do no mighty work where there was unbelief. To handle this weapon correctly means that you must disbelieve everything he says. If he speaks of judgement, care nothing for it; if he speaks of mercy, care nothing for it; if he promises, even swears, that he will do nothing but good to Mansoul if it repents, do not believe him. Question the truth of everything, that is the way to use the shield of unbelief like a true servant of mine.

"Finally, another excellent piece of armour is a prayerless spirit, a spirit that scorns to cry for mercy. Be sure then, my Mansoul, to make use of this. What! Cry for mercy? Never do that, if you would be mine. Why, I know you are all brave men and now, clad in my armour, what need have you to cry to El Shaddai for mercy?"

Having provided his men with armour and weapons, Diabolus concluded with a final word of encouragement:

"Remember, above all else, that *I* am your rightful prince and that you have sworn allegiance to me and my cause. Remember all the kindnesses, the privileges, the immunities and the honours I have shown you. All these call for your loyalty and when could there be so fine an opportunity to show it as now, when another is seeking to take away my dominion over you? Now, if we can but stand together and overcome this one shock, in a little time the whole world will be ours. When that happens, I will make you kings and princes and captains and what splendid times we shall have together then!"

Diabolus, having armed and forearmed his servants in Mansoul against their good and lawful king, then doubled the guards at the gates of the town, himself preparing to defend Heart Castle, his stronghold. The men of Mansoul, to show their gallantry, exercised their weapons every day, defied their enemy and sang the praises of their evil prince, boasting of the great things they would do if ever it should come to a real war between El Shaddai and the tyrant Diabolus.

Chapter Four

El Shaddai sends Deliverance

While all this had been taking place, the good King Shaddai was preparing to send an army to recover the town of Mansoul from the hand of the usurping prince. He decided not to send first by the hand of Emmanuel his son, but by the hand of some of his servants; by them he intended to test the attitude of Mansoul to see whether they would return to the obedience of their true king. The army consisted of more than forty thousand true men, all chosen by the king himself from his own court.[1] These men were

[1] The words of Scripture.

under the charge of four brave captains: Captain Boanerges, Captain Conviction, Captain Judgement and Captain Execution. It was the usual custom of the king, in all his wars, to send these four captains first, for they were very strong, brave men.

Each of these captains was set in charge of ten thousand men and given a banner by the king. *Captain Boanerges*, the chief of the four, had for his standard-bearer Mr. Thunder, who carried the black colours, and his coat-of-arms was three burning thunderbolts. Next came *Captain Conviction*, whose standard-bearer was Mr. Sorrow. He carried the pale colours, his coat-of-arms being the book of the Law, from which issued a flame of fire. Thirdly there was *Captain Judgement*, whose standard-bearer was Mr. Terror. He carried the red colours, with the burning, fiery furnace for his coat-of-arms. Lastly came *Captain Execution*, with Mr. Justice for his standard-bearer, who also carried the red colours, but his coat-of-arms was a fruitless tree, with an axe lying at its root.

When all the men had been mustered and inspected by El Shaddai himself, he delivered to each of the captains their commissions, charging them, in the hearing of all the soldiers, faithfully and courageously to execute all his commands. As all the commissions were the same, only varying slightly in name, title and other minor details, I will give you one as a sample of all.

A commission from the great El Shaddai, king of Mansoul, to his trusty and noble captain, the Captain Boanerges, for his making war upon the town of Mansoul.

"O Boanerges, one of my brave and thundering captains, set in command of ten thousand of my valiant and faithful servants, go in my name, with this force, to the miserable town of Mansoul. When you come there, first offer them conditions of peace, commanding that they cast off the yoke of tyranny of the wicked Diabolus and return to me, their rightful lord; command them also to cleanse themselves from all that belongs to him (and in this you must make quite sure of their obedience). If they submit to your command, you will set up a garrison for me in Mansoul, taking care not to hurt the least person in the town, but to treat them as friends and brothers (for I love them all), telling them that I will soon come and show them how merciful is their king.

"If they resist and rebel, then I command you to use all your wisdom, power and strength to bring them to submission. Farewell."

Having, therefore, received their commissions from the king, the four captains set forth, with flying colours, to march towards the town of Mansoul. Captain Boanerges was in the lead; Captain Conviction and Captain Judgement made up the main body, while Captain Execution brought up the rear. Mansoul was situated a long way from El Shaddai's court, so they travelled through many regions and countries, bringing blessing wherever they went, until at last they arrived at their destination. The captains were greatly saddened when they saw the present condition of Mansoul but, marching right up to the walls, they set themselves down at Ear Gate, the place of hearing, while their men pitched their tents in the plain.

When the people of Mansoul saw such a gallant and well-disciplined company, with its glittering armour and flying colours, they could not resist coming to gaze at this unusual sight. But the cunning Diabolus, fearing that the people might be so overawed at this spectacle that they would suddenly open the gates to the captains, came down quickly from his castle, ordering them all to retire to the centre of the town, where he spoke to them very sternly.

"Gentlemen! Although you are my trusted and well-loved friends, I must reprove you for your curiosity. Do you realise who this company is, or why they have set themselves down before our town in this way? These are the very people I warned you about, some time ago, and against whom I have already tried to arm you, both in body and mind.

"Instead of standing gazing at them, you should have sounded an alarm immediately so that we might all have taken up our positions of defence. As it is, you have made me half-afraid that, when their attack begins, you will give in to them like cowards! Why do you suppose I have commanded you to watch and to set a double guard at your gates? Why have I tried to harden your hearts, till they are like iron, or a mill-stone? Was it so that you might gaze in amazement, like small children, at those who are your mortal enemies?

"Pull yourselves together, beat the drum and present a warlike front, so that our enemies may know that they have brave men to deal with in Mansoul. I will not grumble at you any longer, but take care that I do not again see you acting in this irresponsible manner. No man, without an order from me, is to show his head over the wall of the town. You have heard my words! See that you obey me and all will be well."

As a result of this speech the people of Mansoul were put into a great panic and ran hither and thither through the streets, crying, "Help! Help! The men that turn the world upside down have come here!"

Diabolus was well pleased with their changed attitude and congratulated himself, saying, "Aha! That is what I like to hear. If they will but obey me and keep in *this* frame of mind, I have no fear of any who may try to take this town."

Let us now return to the king's soldiers, who had been lying in wait outside Mansoul. Before three days had passed Captain Boanerges commanded his trumpeter to go down to Ear Gate and there, in the name of the great El Shaddai, to call Mansoul to listen to the message which he would deliver from his master. The trumpeter, whose name was Take-heed-what-you-Hear, went to Ear Gate and sounded his trumpet, but not a soul appeared, or gave any response at all, as Diabolus had commanded. The trumpeter returned to his captain and told how he had been received. This grieved the good captain greatly. However, a little later, Captain Boanerges sent his trumpeter again, but the second time he met with exactly the same reception.

Upon this, the captain and other officers called a council of war to consider what their next steps should be in endeavouring to regain Mansoul for their king. After carefully considering the commissions which they had been given, they decided to give the town a third summons to listen to the king's message. If this still failed to produce a response, then they would endeavour, by force, to compel the men of Mansoul to return to the obedience of their rightful king.

So, for the third time, Take-heed-what-you-Hear went to Ear Gate and, in the name of the king, gave a very loud summons, calling the people of Mansoul to come and listen to the king's noble captains. He added, this time, that if they still refused, the captains intended to come against them and reduce them to obedience by force. This time, however, an answer was forthcoming. Lord Willbewill stood up (you may remember that Diabolus had made him Governor of the Wall and Keeper of the Gates) and, in a pompous and disdainful manner, demanded to know *who* the trumpeter was, *where* he had come from and *why* he was making such a hideous noise and speaking such outrageous words against the town of Mansoul?

The trumpeter answered, "I am servant to the most noble Captain Boanerges, general of the army of the great El Shaddai, against whom you have rebelled, together with the whole town of Mansoul. My master the Captain has a special message for you and for this town. If you will listen peaceably, do so, but if you will not, then you must bear the consequences."

"Very well," said Lord Willbewill, in his most condescending manner, "I will carry your message to Lord Diabolus and will let you know what he says."

"Oh no, you won't," replied the trumpeter. "Our message is not for the giant Diabolus at all, but for the miserable town of Mansoul. We are not the least bit interested in anything *he* may say. We are sent to recover this town from his cruel tyranny and to persuade it to submit, as it did before, to the most excellent El Shaddai."

"Then," said Lord Willbewill, in a more subdued voice, "I will do as you suggest and carry your message to the town."

"Do so," advised the trumpeter, "but do not try any trickery. Be sure of this, that if you do not yield in a peaceable manner, we are quite determined to make war upon you and so bring you to submission. As a proof of my words, to-morrow you will see the black flag, with its burning thunderbolts, raised both as a token of defiance against your prince and of our determination to succeed in the task which our king has committed to us."

Lord Willbewill thereupon departed with his message while the trumpeter returned to the camp and related to the captains how the third summons had been received.

"So far, so good," said Boanerges. "We will lie a little

longer in our trenches and see what these rebels will do."

When the time drew near for Mansoul to give its answer to Boanerges and his captains, he gave order that all the men of war throughout the whole camp should stand together, as one man, ready to receive the town with mercy, if it should surrender, and, if not, to force it into subjection. When daylight came, therefore, the trumpeters sounded throughout the camp, alerting every man to his post, but when the town of Mansoul heard the trumpeters, they were in great consternation, thinking that an attack upon them was beginning, so they also began to prepare for battle.

Having waited until the limit of the appointed time, Captain Boanerges was determined to hear the answer, so he sent his trumpeter once more to summon Mansoul to hear the captain's message. He found, however, that the men of the town had made Ear Gate as secure as they could. Boanerges then called for the Lord Mayor but, when Lord Unbelief showed himself over the wall (he had now been appointed in place of Lord Evil-Desire), Boanerges cried out, "*This* is not the Lord Mayor! Where is Lord Understanding, the original Lord Mayor of Mansoul? It is to him that I will deliver my message."

At this point, Diabolus, who had also come to the wall, shouted out, "Mr. Captain, you have very boldly given Mansoul four summonses to be subject to your king, though I should like to know by whose authority. What do you imagine you are doing by all this?"

Completely ignoring the giant, Captain Boanerges (who had the black colours with the three burning thunderbolts) addressed himself directly to the town of Mansoul.

"Listen to me, O unhappy and rebellious Mansoul. Your most gracious king, the great El Shaddai, my master, has sent me to you with this commission" (this he held up for all to see), "to bring you back again to his obedience. If you yield to my summons, I am to come to you as to my friends and brothers, but if you resist, then I am commanded to subdue you by force."

Then stood forth Captain Conviction (you remember that he had the pale colours with the book of the Law wide open).

"Hear, O Mansoul. Once you were famous for your innocence but now, alas, you are full of lies and deceit. You have heard what my brother, the Captain Boanerges, has said. It would be wise of you, and will make for your happiness, if you will accept the conditions of peace and mercy that have been offered to you, especially when they come from the one against whom you have rebelled, for El Shaddai our king is of great power and none can stand against him when he is angry.

"If you say you have not sinned or rebelled against the king, the whole of your doings since the day you cast off your service to him will speak against you. Why else would you have listened to the tyrant, or received him for your prince? Why else would you reject the laws of El Shaddai and obey this Diabolus? Why else would you shut your gates and take up arms against us, the king's faithful servants? Be advised, then, and accept the Captain's invitation and do not over-step the time of mercy. O Mansoul, do not be held back from mercy, nor allow yourselves to be tricked into a thousand miseries by the deceit of Diabolus. No doubt he will try to make you think that we seek our own advantage in this, but I declare that it is obedience to our king, and a longing for your happiness, that has brought us to you.

"Again, I say, consider what amazing grace it is that causes El Shaddai to humble himself to plead with you, sweetly persuading you, by us, to be reconciled to him. He has no need of you, as you have of him, but you see how merciful he is, not willing that Mansoul should die, but turn to him and live."

When Captain Conviction had concluded, Captain Judgement stood forth (he who had the red colours with the burning fiery furnace), and began:

"O men of Mansoul, who have lived so long in rebellion and treason against your king, understand that we have not come to you in this manner with our own message; it is the king, our master, who has sent us to you. Do not imagine, nor allow the tyrant Diabolus to persuade you, that our king is not able to bring you down by his power, for he is the maker of all things and at his touch the very mountains will smoke. Nor will the gate of his mercy stand open for ever, for the Day of Judgement will surely come and it is coming speedily.

"O Mansoul, is it a small thing in your eyes, that our king offers you mercy, even after so many provocations? *Still* he holds out his golden sceptre to you; *still* he will not allow the gate to be shut against you. Will you provoke him to it? Think well what I say and do not pretend you will never see him for he is ready to judge. Because of his anger, beware that he does not take you away in a moment, for then nothing will deliver you. He has prepared his throne for judgement and will come with fire and in a whirlwind. Therefore, take heed, O Mansoul, take heed, lest justice and judgement should take hold of you!"

(While Captain Judgement was speaking to the town of Mansoul, it was noticed by some that Diabolus began to tremble!) The Captain ended his speech by saying, "O miserable Mansoul, will you not open your gate to receive us, the deputies of your king, who would rejoice to see you saved? Can you endure the judgement that will come upon you? Can you drink the wrath which our king has prepared for Diabolus and his fellows? Consider, O, consider!"

Hereupon, the fourth captain, Captain Execution, began his speech (he also had the red colours depicting the fruitless tree):

"O town of Mansoul, once so fruitful but now like a fruitless branch, once the delight of the noble ones, but now only a den for Diabolus, listen to the words that I shall speak to you in the name of the great El Shaddai. Behold, the axe is laid to the root of the tree, for every tree that brings not forth good fruit is to be hewn down and cast into the fire. You, O Mansoul, are this fruitless tree, for you bear nothing but evil fruit which declares you to be an evil tree. You have rebelled against your king and we, the power and force of El Shaddai, are the axe that is laid to your roots. What do you say? Will you turn before the first blow is given? If I strike you, it will be your end; nothing but yielding to our king can prevent us applying the axe. If mercy does not save you, what are you fit for, but to be hewn down and cast into the fire for burning?

"O Mansoul, patience and forbearance do not last forever. A year, two years, three years perhaps, but, if you rebel for three years (and you have done more than that already) what will follow but 'cut it down . . .'? Do you think these are idle threatenings, or that our king has not power to execute them? O! you will find that in the words of our king, if they are despised by sinners, there is far more than threatening. Your sin has brought this great army to your walls and shall it end in judgement and execution? You have heard what the captains have said, yet still you have shut your gates. Speak, Mansoul! Do you still resist, or will you accept the conditions of peace?"

Mansoul utterly refused to hear the brave speeches of these four noble captains, though some sound of them did beat upon Ear Gate, but not strongly enough to force it open. The town asked for time to prepare an answer, to which the captains replied that if the townsmen would throw out to them old Mr Put-it-Off, they would give them time to answer, but otherwise none; for as long as he was in the town, he would cause nothing but mischief and delay. Diabolus was very unwilling to lose Put-it-Off, as he was one of his ablest spokesmen, so he decided to make answer himself – but then, changing his mind, he commanded the then Lord Mayor, Lord Unbelief, to do it, saying, "My Lord, you give these madmen an answer and speak so that the whole of Mansoul can hear and understand".

Receiving this command, Lord Unbelief began in this manner: "Gentlemen, you have encamped against us and disturbed our peace. Who you are, and where you come from we do not wish to know. You tell us that you come from El Shaddai, though what right he has to send such a message to us we do not know either. You have called upon this town to desert its prince and, for protection, to yield itself up to this same El Shaddai, saying that, in so doing, all past sins will be passed over and forgotten. Further, you have threatened this town with dreadful destructions if it does not obey your commands.

"Now captains, understand that neither Lord Diabolus, nor I his servant, nor any of this brave Mansoul care anything at all for you, your message, or your king. We are not afraid of his power, his greatness or your threats of vengeance and we will *not* yield to his summons. As for this war which you threaten, we shall defend ourselves as best we can. In short, we openly defy you and believe that you have actually deserted your king and are running abroad trying to cause trouble in one town or the next. You will not succeed with Mansoul.

"In conclusion: we are not afraid of you; we shall keep our gates closed against you and we do not wish to be disturbed any more. Begone, or we will attack you ourselves from these walls!"

This defiant speech was seconded by Lord Willbewill: "Gentlemen, we have heard your demands and the noise of your threats, but we are not in the least afraid of you and remain quite unmoved by all that you say. In fact, if you have not departed in three days' time, you will learn what a fearful thing it is to rouse the giant Diabolus when he is asleep in his town of Mansoul."

The Recorder, Mr Forget-Good, then added his little bit: "Gentlemen, with mild and gentle words our lords have answered your rough and angry speeches, when we might have come with force against you. Take their advice and depart quickly, for we are peaceable men and do not really wish to attack you."

Then the town of Mansoul shouted for joy as though they had gained some great victory, and they rang the bells and danced upon the walls. Diabolus returned to his castle and the Lord Mayor and Mr Forget-Good went their ways, but Lord Willbewill took special care that all the gates should be secured with double guards and double bolts and bars. So that Ear Gate might be especially protected (for here the king's forces would be most eager to enter) he made Mr Prejudice, an angry unpleasant old man, captain of the soldiers there. Under his power he put sixty deaf men, most suitable for the particular work of protecting Ear Gate against the attacks of the king's army.

Chapter Five

Fightings Without and Fears Within

When the captains saw what answer they could expect from the chief men of the town, that they could not get a hearing from the ordinary townsmen and that Mansoul was determined to resist, they prepared themselves for battle. First, they greatly strengthened their force at Ear Gate, for they knew that they must penetrate here or no good could come to the town. This done, they put the remainder of their men in their places, sounded the trumpet and gave out the battle-cry, "*Ye must be born again*". Those in the town answered them, shout for shout and charge against charge, and so the battle began.

The men of Mansoul had two huge guns in which they greatly trusted called Heady and High-Mind. These they set upon the tower over Ear Gate, but the captains were so vigilant and watchful that, although the shots from these guns sometimes whizzed by their ears, yet they were unharmed. The townsmen hoped, with these guns, to do much damage to the camp of El Shaddai, but they were really quite ineffective.

The captains' men attacked the town with great valour, particularly trying to break open Ear Gate, for they knew that if they failed there it would be useless to batter the wall. They used several battering rams and some slings and there were many skirmishes and encounters. But Mansoul resisted so strongly, upheld by the rage of Diabolus and the determination of Lord Willbewill, Unbelief and Forget-Good that, for that summer, it seemed as though the king's forces were quite beaten and the advantage remained with Mansoul. When the captains saw how the position lay, they called a retreat and entrenched themselves for the winter. There were some losses sustained on both sides, which I will mention to you briefly.

I did not tell you before that, as Boanerges and his army were marching across the country toward Mansoul, they came upon three young men who desired to enlist as soldiers. They were very presentable fellows, called Mr Tradition, Mr Human-Wisdom and Mr Man's-own-Ideas, who offered their services to the king's officers. The captains faithfully warned them of the dangers that were likely to be encountered in this attack which was planned against Diabolus and that they should think well before committing themselves. The men insisted, however, that their minds were quite made up and that they were eager to serve the great El Shaddai. Seeing that they were apparently men of some skill and courage, Captain Boanerges agreed to enlist them in his company and away they marched to the war.

Now, during one of the skirmishes recently referred to, Lord Willbewill's men sallied forth from the town and, attacking Boanerges' men from the rear, captured these three men – Mr Tradition, Mr Human-Wisdom and Mr Man's-own-Ideas – taking them back into the town as prisoners-of-war. When Diabolus learned of this, he sent for the men to be brought before him in the castle where he questioned them carefully, wanting to know how they came to be serving El Shaddai. He then asked if they would be willing to serve him against their former captains.

"O yes," they replied quite cheerfully. "We do not really live strictly by religion but rather by the fates of fortune and, since we are now in your hands, we would be just as happy to serve your lordship as we were to serve under the king."

Being pleased at gaining the service of such useful men, Diabolus (after leaving them in prison for a few more days) sent them with a note from himself to Captain Anything, a very obliging officer of his in the town.

"My dear adaptable Anything," said the note, "I am sending you three fine young men to serve under you, adaptable as yourself, and I am sure you will be able to make good use of them in one position or another."

These men, therefore, were lost to the service of the king, but the king's men did some damage to the enemy. In one attack from the slings, they broke open the roof of Lord Unbelief's palace. At another time, Lord Willbewill was almost killed outright, but he somehow managed to recover; while, with only one shot from the slings, several of the aldermen were killed instantly – Mr Swearing, Mr Fury, Mr Cheating, Mr Quick-to-Lie and Mr Drunkenness. They also dismounted the two great guns, Heady and High-Mind, that stood on the tower above Ear Gate, laying them flat in the dirt.

Now to return to the camp. During the cold and dreary winter months the king's captains kept up continual alarms and disturbances, first at this gate, then at that, then at all five of them at once, so that the town of Mansoul was no longer left in peace, as before, to pursue its sins and pleasures. Sometimes thousands of the soldiers would be running round the walls of the town at midnight, shouting their battle-cry. Sometimes the slings would whirl a hail of stones over the walls, when the cries of the wounded could be heard all over the town. No doubt even Diabolus himself had his rest disturbed as he lay in his castle.

Because of all these happenings, new thoughts began to run through the city and possess the minds of the men of Mansoul. Some would be heard saying, "This is terrible! We cannot go on living like this!"

Others would say, "O it will pass, it will pass". Yet others would say, "Let us turn again to King Shaddai and so put an end to all our troubles". Then a fourth would add, "But we do not know whether he will receive us now. We have left it too late, I fear."

Now, also, Mr Conscience, the previous Recorder, began to talk loudly and his words came like tremendous thunder-claps, to add to the noise and shouting of the soldiers and the alarm calls of the captains.

In addition to all these troubles a famine began to arise, for many of the pleasant things in which the people delighted began to grow scarce. O how glad would Mansoul have been now for a little peace and quietness of mind, but Captain Boanerges sent his trumpeter with a summons commanding Mansoul to yield to the king. Three times he was sent forth in the hope that, by now, there might be some amongst the townsmen who would be willing to surrender, given a new invitation to do so. In point of fact, the town would have surrendered itself up long ago, had it not been for the opposition of Lord Unbelief and Lord Willbewill. Diabolus, also, began to rave again and so Mansoul was divided in its mind and lay continually in a state of distress and fear.

The first of the summonses just referred to reminded the town of the king's readiness to forgive and show mercy if Mansoul would humbly turn to him. The second summons was phrased a little more roughly, warning the town that, however long it held out against them, the captains were absolutely determined to succeed. Taking the third summons, the trumpeter said that he did not know whether the captains were inclining now towards mercy or judgement, but they still commanded that the gates be opened to them.

These three summonses, especially the last two, so worried the town that, after consultation, it was decided to send Lord Willbewill to Ear Gate, with a trumpeter, to call the captains for a parley. When the captains arrived, with all their men in attendance, the townsmen said that they would come to an agreement with King Shaddai on the following terms, which their prince had allowed them to offer:

(I) That Lord Unbelief, Lord Willbewill and Mr Forget-Good should, under El Shaddai, still be the governors of the town of Mansoul.

(II) That no man now serving under Diabolus should be cast out of the town or lose his freedom.

(III) That the townsmen might still retain all the privileges they had enjoyed under the reign of Diabolus.

(IV) That no new law, or officer of the law, should have any power over them without their previous choice and consent.

"These are our conditions of surrender," said the townsmen, "and upon these we are prepared to submit ourselves to you."

You can imagine how these terms were received by the noble Captain Boanerges! He immediately addressed the town in the following manner: "O inhabitants of Mansoul, when I first heard your trumpeter calling for a parley I was truly glad, and when you agreed to submit yourselves to our lord and king I was even more glad. But now I am filled with sadness, having heard your bold and foolish conditions. Surely I detect the hand of that rascal Put-it-Off in these terms! Such conditions could *never* be listened to for one moment by any true servant of El Shaddai and we utterly reject and disdain them. But, O Mansoul, if you will only give yourselves into the hands of our king, trusting him to make such terms that will seem good to him (and would certainly be for your advantage) then we will receive you. Otherwise, we are back where we started and we know what we shall do!"

At this, old Lord Unbelief cried out, "Who do you suppose would be so foolish as to put himself into the hands of his enemy? What do we know of the temper of this king? 'Tis said by some that he is angry with his subjects if they are even a hair's breadth out of line and, by others, that he demands more than anyone can perform. Take heed what you do, O Mansoul. How do you know, when you are his, which of us he may kill, or whether he may not kill every one of us and fill this town with new people?"

This speech, of course, undid everything and put an end to any hope of success from the parley. The captains returned to their trenches and the Lord Mayor to the castle. Diabolus was waiting for his return in the chamber of state and, upon hearing Unbelief's account of the parley, he said, "My Lord Mayor, my dear Unbelief, you have served me well in this matter. You have proved your loyalty so many times and you have never yet failed me. When we have brought this little affair to a satisfactory conclusion, I will honour your faithfulness, promoting you to a position far superior to that of Lord Mayor of Mansoul. You shall be my universal deputy and have all nations under your power."

The Lord Mayor left the presence of Diabolus in a most happy frame of mind, congratulating himself on the favours which he hoped eventually to receive, but he little knew that Mansoul was now in a state of mutiny. For, while he had been in the castle conferring with the prince, the previous Lord Mayor, Lord Understanding, and the previous Recorder, Mr Conscience, having somehow heard what had been taking place at Ear Gate, began to talk to some of the townsmen, pointing out the rudeness shown to the captains and their king. The multitude of the people, now fearing what would come of Unbelief's rough speech, began to run about, saying quite openly, "O! the brave captains of El Shaddai! O that we were under the government of the captains and of their noble king!"

Hearing eventually of this uproar, Lord Unbelief came quickly from his house, expecting to quell the people easily with a show of his dignity, but when they saw him, they came running at him and would have done him a serious injury had he not hastened, like a scared rabbit, back to his house. The townsmen even tried to attack his house but it was too strong for them. Meanwhile, Unbelief went upstairs in order that he might safely address the people from a window. "Men of Mansoul," he began, "what is the meaning of this uproar in the town today?"

"The uproar has been caused," replied Lord Understanding, "because you have not given a correct reply to the captains of El Shaddai. You have offered them terms which are utterly unacceptable, terms which are, in fact, nothing more than an insult, and you have repulsed their offers of mercy and forgiveness. You are an enemy to this town, sir."

"Treason! Treason!" cried Unbelief. "To arms, O you trusty men of Mansoul!"

"Sir," answered Lord Understanding, "you may call it treason if you wish, but I am sure that the captains of such a great lord as theirs deserved a better answer."

"What I spoke," replied Unbelief haughtily, "I spoke for my master Diabolus, on behalf of the ignorant people of this town, whom you have stirred up into a state of mutiny."

"As to that," joined in Mr Conscience, "it is evident that Lord Understanding states the truth and that you are an enemy of Mansoul. If you had accepted the captains' conditions of peace, the sound of the trumpet and the alarm of war would now have ended. As it is, they are still upon us and we have your rude and stupid speech to thank for that."

Lord Unbelief was highly affronted at this and replied, "I shall now go and tell Lord Diabolus of your words. He will know how to make you sorry for them. Know also that he and I will continue to seek the good of this town without asking your advice."

"Will you, indeed?" answered Lord Understanding. "My opinion is that since you, sir, and your prince are not natives of this town, having brought us into these desperate conditions, you may well take flight, for all we know, and leave us to fend for ourselves."

While this argument was taking place, down from the walls and gates of the town came Lord Willbewill, Mr Prejudice and old Put-it-Off, with several of the aldermen, to ask the reason for the tumult. Everyone began to speak at once, so that nothing but confusion prevailed.

When there was a slight pause, the sly and crafty Lord

Unbelief said, "My Lord, there are a couple of peevish men here, namely Lord Understanding and Mr Conscience, who, at the advice of Mr Discontent, have aroused these people against me and are now trying to incite them to rebel against our prince Diabolus."

All the Diabolonians present sided with old Unbelief, confirming his lying story, praising up Diabolus and at the same time shouting for Mr Conscience and Lord Understanding to be cast into prison, while those on the other side praised up El Shaddai and his laws, his mercy and his captains. Soon the bickering changed to blows and many people were hurt. Good old Mr Conscience was knocked down twice and Lord Understanding would have been shot in the head, only the marksman's aim was rather poor! Of the Diabolonians, Mr Rash-Head had his brains knocked out by Mr Mind (Willbewill's clerk) and it was quite funny to see old Mr Prejudice rolling in the mud. Captain Anything was eager to join in, but both sides were against him because he was true to neither of them. He ended up by having one of his legs broken (and the man who did it wished it had been his neck!). Lord Willbewill acted rather strangely in all this, as though he did not know which side he was on, but it was noticeable that he laughed aloud when he saw Mr Prejudice knocked down and completely ignored Captain Anything when he came struggling up before him.

When the uproar had subsided, Diabolus threw Lord Understanding and Mr Conscience into prison, charging them with being the ring-leaders of the disturbance. The town quietened down at last and the two prisoners had rather a bad time; in fact, the evil prince would have killed them to get them once and for all out of his way but, with war at the very gates, he thought it better to postpone dealing with them for a little while.

Chapter Six

Emmanuel rides forth to Conquer

The persevering captains held another council of war and decided to send yet one more summons to the town, feeling sure that there were now many who were inclined to yield. This time the trumpeter, going straight to Ear Gate, spoke of the greatness of El Shaddai and his marvellous works, urging the townsmen to reject the lies and falsehoods of Diabolus, and to accept the golden offers of the king.

"Do you think," he continued, "that you are stronger than he – you, who are as grasshoppers in his sight? Consider the heavens and the stars, the works of his fingers. Consider the sun and the moon, how he keeps them steadfastly shining in their places. Consider the mighty oceans, which he is able to keep in bounds. Consider how small and puny and insignificant you are in comparison with him. Remember that it is in the name of such a great one that I come to you today, commanding your surrender."

The men of Mansoul were rather affected by this speech and did not quite know what to answer. But Diabolus quickly appeared and turned the greatness of El Shaddai, of which the trumpeter had been speaking, into something that would make the people tremble.

"Gentlemen," he said, addressing the men of Mansoul, "you have heard the wonderful things which the messenger has spoken of his king. Assuming that he speaks the truth, imagine what bondage this great king will keep you in for ever. If you are afraid to think of him while he is at a distance, how do you suppose you will feel when he is in your midst, as your king? *I* do not try to make you tremble, for I am friendly and familiar with you. Therefore, think carefully and consider what will be for your profit."

The result of this speech was to make the townsmen harden their hearts even further against the king. Thoughts of his greatness filled them with dread, while thoughts of his holiness reduced them to despair. Because of this, they sent word back to the captains by the trumpeter, that they had resolved to stick to their prince, Diabolus, that they would never, never yield to El Shaddai and that it was a waste of time to send any more summonses.

The upshot of all this was that the captains decided that Mansoul would have to be won by some other method. They held a conference, suggesting first this and then that, until finally Captain Conviction stood up and said, "My brother captains, my advice is that we continue to keep the town in a state of alarm, by day and by night, but at the same time send a petition to our King Shaddai, telling him how we have fared and begging his pardon that we have not had better success. Let us also implore him to send us reinforcements, with some gallant and well-spoken commander to head them, so that our king may not lose the benefit of the beginnings we have made, but may complete the conquest of the town."

It was agreed that this was an excellent idea and the petition was drawn up as follows:

"Most gracious and glorious king, builder of the town of Mansoul, at your command we, your faithful servants, have made war upon your town of Mansoul seeking to subdue it for your majesty. First, we offered conditions of peace, but the inhabitants made light of this, shutting their gates and mounting their guns. The tyrant prince, Diabolus, Lord Unbelief and Lord Willbewill are our greatest opponents. Had there been one friend within its walls to second our summons, we might have succeeded, but, up to the present moment, the town continues in its rebellion.

"Now, O king, pardon our lack of success and send us, we pray, more forces under the command of a man whom the town may both love and fear. Amen."

This petition was speedily despatched to the king, the messenger being a good man called Mr Love-to-Mansoul. When he arrived at the king's palace he delivered it into the very hands of the king's son, Emmanuel, who read it through and, being very pleased with its contents, added a few things to it himself and then carried it to his father. The king, El Shaddai, received the petition with gladness, especially as it was seconded by his well-beloved son. He was also pleased to hear of his servants' determination and of the beginnings that had been made against Mansoul. Calling his son, Emmanuel, to him he said, "You know well, as I do, the condition of Mansoul: what we have purposed together to do for it and what you have already accomplished yourself to redeem it. Come my son, *you* shall go to my camp at Mansoul, for there you will prosper and conquer the town."

Then Emmanuel answered, "Your law is within my heart, and I delight to do your will, O my father. This is the work that I long to do. Give me such forces as you think fit and I will go and deliver this perishing town of Mansoul out of the hand of the tyrant Diabolus. I have often been grieved to hear of its misery and decay and nothing will give me greater joy than to bring about its deliverance. Nothing is too dear for my people of Mansoul and I am delighted to be made the captain of their salvation".

News of this flew round the king's court like lightning and all were talking of the gracious things that Emmanuel intended to do for Mansoul. The highest nobles in the court desired to have a commission and to go with their prince on his conquest. When tidings came to the men encamped around Mansoul that Emmanuel himself was coming to their aid, with a force so great that it could not be resisted, the captains and their men sent forth such a shout of joy that the earth shook, the mountains answered by their echo and Diabolus himself began greatly to shake and tremble – and for this good reason. Although Mansoul itself cared little about this project, being quite taken up with its pleasure-seeking and sin, yet Diabolus, its governor, was very much afraid. His spies were abroad everywhere, bringing him news of many things, and one soon arrived at the castle who brought him word of what had taken place in the king's court, namely that Emmanuel himself was soon coming against him! – and there was no-one that Diabolus feared so much as this great prince. He had already suffered much at his hand and he dreaded to hear even the mention of his name.

The time had now come for Emmanuel to leave his father's court and begin his march towards Mansoul. Here I must pause to tell you of the five brave captains who accompanied him.

First, there was the famous *Captain Faith*. He had the red colours, carried by Mr Promise and his coat-of-arms was the holy lamb and the golden shield. Next came the equally famous *Captain Good-Hope*, with the blue colours carried by Mr Expectation, his coat-of-arms being the three golden anchors. Thirdly came that gracious *Captain Love*, with Mr Compassion carrying the green colours. On his shield were depicted three naked orphans held in a loving embrace. After this came the gallant *Captain Purity*. His colours, which were white, were carried by Mr Harmless and on his shield were three golden doves. Finally came the well-beloved *Captain Patience*, whose colours were black. Mr Long-Suffering was his standard-bearer and his coat-of-arms showed three arrows piercing through a heart of gold.

These were Emmanuel's captains and in this order they marched, each with his ten thousand men – Captain Faith leading, Captain Patience in the rear and the prince himself riding at the head of his army in his chariot.

O! what a splendid sight they were as they marched forth, with the trumpets sounding, their armour glittering and their colours waving gaily in the wind. The prince's armour was made entirely of burnished gold and shone like the sun in the heavens, while the captains' armour glittered like the stars. Within the heart of the army, they carried fifty-four battering rams and twelve slings, all made of the purest gold.[1]

On and on they marched, until they came within about three miles of the town. Here they halted, waited for the first four captains to come out and greet their prince, after

[1] These are the sixty-six books of the Bible.

which they all journeyed on together toward Mansoul. When the soldiers, who had been in the camp from the beginning, saw the reinforcements that had come to join them, *and* their prince at their head, they again gave such a shout of rejoicing that it put Diabolus in another great fright. The old and new forces then set themselves down, completely surrounding the town, so that now, whichever way it might look, Mansoul was besieged.

When the men of the town saw the vast array of soldiers set against them and the golden slings and battering rams, when they saw the glittering armour gleaming on every side and the waving colours, they were filled with fear. For, although they thought themselves to be very well defended, they began to wonder just what would be the outcome of all this.

The town now being completely surrounded, the good prince Emmanuel set up the white flag to hang among the golden slings, and this for two reasons: first, to show that he could and would be gracious if Mansoul would yet turn to him and, secondly, to leave them without excuse, should he destroy them because of their continued rebellion. So the white flag, with the three golden doves, hung there for two days but the town made no reply to this signal. Then the prince caused the red flag to be hung, the flag of Captain Judgement, with the fiery furnace depicted on it. This, also, hung for several days, but again the townspeople made no reply. Finally, Emmanuel commanded that the black flag of defiance, with the three burning thunderbolts, be hung forth, but again, Mansoul was apparently still unmoved.

Seeing that neither mercy, nor judgement, nor execution of judgement, could move the rebellious town, the tender-hearted prince was filled with pity, saying to his captains, "Surely their strange behaviour is due to their ignorance of the ways of war, rather than to secret defiance".

So he sent to the town, to let them know the meaning of the flags, and to know whether they would choose grace and mercy, or judgement, and the execution of judgement. All this time the gates were kept fast shut and the guards were doubled, while Diabolus encouraged his people in their resistance as much as he possibly could. The townspeople then sent answer to the prince:

"Great Sir, with regard to your message, whether we will accept of your mercy, or fall by your justice, we can give you no positive answer. It is against the law and government of our prince for us to make either peace or war without him but we will ask him to come to the wall and speak to you on our behalf."

Emmanuel was greatly grieved, as he always was, to see the slavery and bondage of the people and how content they were to remain in the chains of the tyrant. Diabolus was secretly very much afraid when he heard the townspeople's answer, but reluctantly agreed to go and speak to the prince at Mouth Gate. This is what he said (but in a language which the town could not understand):

"O great Emmanuel, lord of all the world, I know who you are, the son of the great El Shaddai. Why have you come to torment me and cast me out of my lawful possession? This town of Mansoul is mine, as you very well know, and for two good reasons. It is mine by right of conquest, because I won it in open battle. Why should I yield up my prey? It is mine because the townspeople willingly gave themselves to me, opening their gates, choosing me for their prince and giving Heart Castle willingly into my hand.

"Moreover, they have turned against you and cast your law, your name, your image and all that is yours behind their backs and they have accepted my law, my name, my image and all that is mine. Ask your captains. They will tell you that Mansoul has answered all their summonses by showing love and faithfulness to me and disdain and contempt to you and yours. Since you pride yourself on your justice and holiness, depart, I pray you, and leave me with my rightful possession."

This speech, you must remember, was made in Diabolus's own language, which Mansoul could not understand; neither could they see how he crouched and cringed before Emmanuel, their true prince. They still imagined, poor, deluded souls, that he was exceedingly brave and strong and one to be greatly reckoned with.

When the upstart prince had finished speaking Emmanuel, the golden prince, stood up and replied to him in this manner:

"O you deceiver, in my father's name and my own name and on behalf of this wretched town of Mansoul, I have something to say to you. Although you are pretending a lawful right to this town, it is most apparent to all my father's court that you have only obtained entrance by lies and deceit.

"You have lied about my father and his law, and have thereby deceived my people of Mansoul. You pretend that they have accepted you as their prince, but this, again, was only through your trickery. You promised these innocent people happiness in breaking my father's commandments, although you knew full well, from your own bitter experience, that this would be their undoing and misery. You have, in great contempt and spite to my father, defaced his image in Mansoul and set up your own in its place. You have stirred up my people against their deliverance and set them against my father's captains. I am come to avenge the lies you have spoken of my father and the terrible wrong you have done to this town and I intend to bring down your evil doings upon your own head.

"As for myself, I have come against you with lawful

power to retrieve this town of Mansoul out of your cruel clutches, for it is *mine*, and this I will prove to your own confusion.

"First, this town was built by my father with his own hand and the palace in the midst of it he built for his personal delight. Secondly, this town is mine because I am my father's heir, and the delight of his heart. Therefore, this town is my inheritance. It was originally given to me by my father as a gift and it is yet my desire, my delight and the joy of my heart.

"It is also mine by right of purchase, O Diabolus, for I have bought it for myself. Mansoul sinned against my father by listening to your lying voice and yielding to your temptations; and he had already said that in the day that they broke his law, they should die. Now it is more possible for heaven and earth to pass away, than that he should break his word. Therefore, when Mansoul sinned, I pledged myself to my father to make amends for its transgression, for no reason but that I have set my love upon this town. When the appointed time had come, I gave body for body, soul for soul, blood for blood, and so I redeemed my beloved Mansoul. By this, my father's law and justice are now both satisfied and well content that Mansoul should be delivered.

"Finally, be it known unto you, that I have come out against you by the express command of my father.

"And now," concluded the prince, "I have a word for the town of Mansoul."

The moment he said this, however, the gates were treble-guarded and the men ordered not to listen.

"O unhappy Mansoul," continued the prince, "I am full of pity and compassion for you. You have accepted Diabolus for your prince, against your true sovereign lord. Your gates were opened to him, but they are shut against me. He brought you destruction and you received him; I bring you salvation, yet you will not listen to me. You have given yourself into the hand of my father's greatest enemy. Poor Mansoul! What shall I do to you? It is not my intention to hurt you, yet you fly from me. This great force that is with me is not for your hurt, but for your deliverance. My commission is to make war upon Diabolus and his followers, not upon yourselves, for he is the strong man armed, keeping his goods in peace, but I will have him out!

"All my words are true and you shall know this when you see him following me in chains, for I *will* deliver you, Mansoul, out of his hand, I, who am mighty to save."

This wonderful speech was addressed to the town of Mansoul, but they would not hear it. So horribly were these townsmen enchanted by Diabolus, that they locked and bolted and barricaded Ear Gate over and over again, so that they should not hear one word from outside.

Chapter Seven

Diabolus Disgraced and Driven Forth

When Emmanuel saw, therefore, that Mansoul was so utterly involved in sin that all his gracious words were despised, he gave a command for his forces to be ready at a certain time. The battering rams and slings he ordered to be set against Ear Gate and Eye Gate, since there was no other way lawfully to take the town. Before engaging in battle, however, the prince sent once more to see if the town would yield peaceably, or whether they were still determined to resist to the bitter end. The chief men of Mansoul held a council of war with Diabolus and decided to send certain propositions to Emmanuel to see if he would accept them. These were sent by the hand of that stiff old man Mr Will-not-Stoop, who was told exactly what he was to say. Arriving at the royal camp, he asked for an audience with the prince and, this being granted, addressed him in the following manner:

Will-not-Stoop: "Great Sir, so that all may see how good-natured our master is, he has sent me to tell your lordship that he is willing, rather than go to war, to deliver into your hands one half of the town of Mansoul. Will your mightiness accept this proposition?"

Emmanuel: "The whole of Mansoul is mine, by gift and purchase, therefore I will not lose one half."

Will-not-Stoop: "Sir, my master will be content that you should be lord, in title, if he may rule but a part."

Emmanuel: "The whole is mine in actual fact, not in name only. I will be lord of all, or of nothing, in Mansoul."

Will-not-Stoop: "My gracious master says he will be content for you to be lord, if he may have a small place to live in privately."

Emmanuel: "No, I will not allow him the least corner of Mansoul to dwell in; I will have it all to myself."

Will-not-Stoop: "Suppose my master resigns the whole town to you, on condition that for old time's sake, he may stay for visits of two, or ten days, or perhaps a month?"

Emmanuel: "No, I will not agree that he should ever enter the city again, for any reason whatsoever."

Will-not-Stoop: "Sir, you are very hard. You will at least allow that my master's friends and relations should still stay to dwell and trade in the town?"

Emmanuel: "No, that is contrary to my father's will. Every Diabolonian now in Mansoul or at any future time found within this town shall lose, not only his land and liberty, but also his life."

Will-not-Stoop: "But, Sir, you will surely allow my master, by letter and chance opportunities, to keep up some of his old friendship with Mansoul?"

Emmanuel: "No, by no means. Any such friendship will only lead to the corruption of Mansoul, and will take their affections away from my father and me."

Will-not-Stoop: "Then, great Sir, if my master altogether departs, surely he may leave some gifts, to remind the people of their old friend and of the merry times they had together while he was their prince?"

Emmanuel: "No, indeed. When Mansoul is mine, I will not allow the least scrap or shred or dust of Diabolus to be left to remind them of the horrible alliance they once made with him."

Will-not-Stoop: "Well, Sir, I have one more thing to mention and then I have finished. Suppose, when my master has left this town, that some difficulty arises, which only he could solve? May he and the persons concerned meet and put their heads together, to see how to act in such a case?"

Emmanuel: "No, certainly not. There can never arise a difficulty or matter which my father cannot solve, and all in Mansoul will be instructed that in everything, by prayer and supplication, their requests are to be made known to him alone."

Having received this unyielding answer, Mr Will-not-Stoop returned to Diabolus to tell him that when once he, Diabolus, had left the town, Emmanuel would never again allow him to have the slightest relationship with his people at all. Upon hearing all this, Diabolus and the townsmen immediately agreed to do everything possible to keep

Emmanuel out. They sent old Mr Put-it-Off once again, this time to tell the prince and his captains that Diabolus and Mansoul had resolved to stand or fall together, and that Emmanuel should never possess Mansoul unless he could take it by force.

"So then," said the prince, "by this I am compelled to show them the power of my sword, for I am determined to deliver my Mansoul from the hand of the enemy."

He then placed his captains at different stations round the town, the battle cry "*Emmanuel*" went forth, the alarm was raised and the slings and the battering rams set in action. Diabolus greatly encouraged his men at every gate and they put up a forcible resistance, which continued for some days.

During the first part of the battle, Emmanuel's captains succeeded in shaking, and almost breaking down, Ear Gate and Eye Gate. Many of the Diabolonian captains, amongst them Captain Boasting and Captain Bragman, were killed and others severely wounded. Captain Anything and old Mr Prejudice fled into hiding; Mr Feeling was severely wounded in the eye and made a hasty retreat, while Mr Put-it-Off had his head cracked open. Lord Willbewill received a severe injury to his leg which handicapped him considerably, hindering him, for the first time in years, from doing just what he wanted. He was seen afterwards, by some of the captains' men, to be limping very badly.

When this part of the battle was over, the prince again commanded the white flag to be raised to show that he yet had grace for Mansoul. Diabolus saw this and knew full well that it was not for him; but he thought he would try another trick to see if the prince would raise the siege and go, if a promise of reformation were given. So one evening, after sunset, he came down to the gate and called to speak with Emmanuel, who consented to come and see him.

"Since you have raised the white flag and shown that you are peaceably inclined," began the cunning prince, "I thought I would come and tell you of the terms on which we will surrender. I know that you are doing all this to make Mansoul a holy place. Well, call off your forces and I will make the townspeople do as you wish. I will be your deputy, for I can easily make Mansoul submit to you. I will show them where they have sinned against you and insist that they must now reform themselves. I will show them your holy law and tell them that this must be kept. I will, at my own cost, maintain a company of lecturers to teach the people your ways; and every year we will pay whatever taxes you think fit, because we are your subjects!"

To this fine speech, Emmanuel replied, "O you deceitful one! How you do change and change again. These proposals of yours are no better than the first. Having failed in your natural form, are you now trying to disguise yourself as an angel of light and as a minister of righteousness?

"When will you understand that nothing you suggest will be considered? You have no conscience toward El Shaddai my father nor love toward the town of Mansoul. You talk now of reformation, when you know full well that, having once broken the law Mansoul can never be restored by its own attempts at righteousness. (I will say nothing of the fine sort of righteousness that would be produced by the townspeople with you, O evil one, as their teacher!) I have not come to urge Mansoul to live by works, but that by me and what I have done and shall do, Mansoul may be reconciled to my father, though by their sin they have provoked him to anger and by the law they cannot obtain mercy.

"You talk boldly of reforming this town when you know well enough that no-one within it desires such a thing. I am sent by my father to possess it for myself that, by the skilful guiding of my hand I may make it, once again, pleasing in his sight. I will cast you out and I will govern with new laws, new officers, new motives and new ways. I will pull this town down and build it again, so that it will be altogether glorious!"

His deceitfulness now being exposed, Diabolus was once more filled with violent rage and strengthened himself to give battle afresh against the noble Emmanuel. (Now watch and see how the fatal blow is eventually given, while one seeks to hold and the other seeks to make himself master of Mansoul.)

Despairing of any longer retaining Mansoul for himself, Diabolus determined to do as much damage within it as possible; for it was not the happiness of the silly town he desired, but rather its utter ruin and destruction. He ordered his soldiers, therefore, to tear men, women and children to pieces and demolish the place so that, when Emmanuel finally took it, there would be nothing for him but a ruinous heap.

Emmanuel, on the other hand, knowing that this battle would result in his becoming master of the town, gave out a royal command to all his officers and men to fight to the utmost against Diabolus and his Diabolonians, but to be merciful, pitiful and gentle to the true inhabitants of the town.

"Make certain," he commanded, "that the hottest part of the battle be directed always against the Diabolonians."

At break of day the battle was renewed, the battle-cry this time being "*Mansoul is won*" and the prince's men set all their might against Ear Gate and Eye Gate. For a while, Diabolus fought very fiercely against the prince's army but at length, after three or four mighty charges, Ear Gate was broken open, its bars and bolts shattering into a thousand pieces. At this, the silver trumpets sounded, the captains shouted, the townspeople shivered in their shoes and the giant retreated hastily to his castle.

Emmanuel immediately entered the town, setting up his throne and his royal standard, temporarily, in that very gate. The golden slings were brought in, at his command, and directed upon the castle itself, this being where Diabolus was now hiding.

From Ear Gate the road went straight to Mr Conscience's house, which lies directly opposite the castle. Therefore, three of the first four captains who had come against Mansoul, namely Captain Boanerges, Captain Conviction and Captain Judgement, at Emmanuel's command, marched straight up to the Recorder's house (which was nearly as strong as a castle) and demanded entrance. (I did not tell you, but Mr Conscience and Lord Understanding, unknown to Diabolus, managed to escape from prison in the general uproar and confusion, and Mr Conscience was now back in his own house again.) At first, the old man was too afraid to answer, but when one stroke of the battering-ram made the whole building tremble and totter, he came to his gate and, with quivering lips, asked who was there. Boanerges answered that they were the captains and commanders of the great El Shaddai and his blessed son Emmanuel, and that they demanded possession of his house for their noble prince. At this, the battering-ram gave the gate another shake and, although poor Mr Conscience was trembling all over, he dared do nothing else but open to the captains. (Because of its position, as I have just explained, this house was an excellent place from which to make an attack upon Heart Castle.)

Mr Conscience did not know what to think of all this and when some of the townspeople, hearing that his house had been taken over by the captains, came to see him, he could talk of nothing but death and destruction.

"For," said the trembling old gentleman, "you are well aware that we have all been traitors to the once despised and now gloriously victorious Prince Emmanuel. He has forced his way into our gates and the mighty Diabolus flees before him. For myself, I know that I have sinned greatly by keeping silent when I should have spoken and by perverting justice when I should have been diligent to carry it out. True, I have suffered somewhat at the hands of Diabolus for speaking at times of the laws of El Shaddai, but that will hardly make amends for all the things I have neglected to do or the treasonable things I have said. O, I tremble to think what will be the end of all this!"

While the three captains before mentioned were engaged with Mr Conscience, Captain Execution was busy on the walls and in the back streets of the town. He hunted out Lord Willbewill, pursuing him mercilessly and, although he managed to hide at length, several of Willbewill's officers were felled to the ground by this brave captain. Old Mr Prejudice was killed outright and so was Captain Treacherous, while Mr Put-it-Off, who had done much mischief in the town, fell by the hand of Captain Good-Hope. Altogether, many Diabolonians were killed or severely wounded, but not one true native of Mansoul was hurt at all. Indeed, there were Diabolonians lying dead in every corner – but there were still far too many left alive for the good of Mansoul.

At this point, the old Recorder, Mr Conscience, Lord Understanding, Lord Willbewill and several others of the chief men of Mansoul, knowing that they must stand or fall with the town, agreed together to draw up a petition and send it to Emmanuel while he still sat in the gate. It was quite short, saying very simply, "We, the old inhabitants of Mansoul, confess our sin, being very sorry that we have offended your princely majesty and beg that you will spare our lives. Amen".

To this petition the prince gave no answer at all which, naturally, troubled the town a great deal.

While this was taking place, the captains in Mr Conscience's house were continuing to attack Heart Castle with the battering-rams until, after some time and trouble, the main gate at last broke into splinters, laying open the way into the castle where Diabolus was hiding. News was immediately sent to Emmanuel and O! how the trumpets sounded forth, now that the end of the war was actually in sight.

Then Emmanuel arose and, taking with him some of his ablest men, marched straight up the main street of Mansoul toward the house of Mr Conscience. The prince was clad in armour of purest gold and his royal standard was carried before him; but he kept his face very set and stern as he went, so that the townspeople could not tell what to expect from him. They all came to the doors to see him pass and were quite overcome at the sight of his glorious person – but rather troubled at his expression. For the present time he preferred to speak to them by his deeds and actions, rather than with words or smiles; but poor Mansoul thought, "If the prince loved us, surely he would show it in his face; therefore, he must hate us, and we shall all be slain", for they realised that the prince knew all the terrible story of their wickedness and rebellion. As Emmanuel went past, they bowed very, very humbly before him and then began to talk amongst themselves of the glory of his person, the dignity of his bearing and how they wished, a thousand times over, that he would become their prince and protector.

Arriving at the castle gate, Emmanuel commanded Diabolus to appear and surrender himself to his victor. O! how unwilling was this tyrant to show himself; but at length out he came, scowling and cursing. He was immediately bound fast in chains and taken by the prince to the market-place where, before all Mansoul, Emmanuel stripped him of his armour of which he had boasted so much. All this time the trumpets of the golden prince were sounding forth and his captains and soldiers were shouting and singing for joy. In this way Mansoul was called upon to watch the beginning of Emmanuel's triumph over this tyrant of whom they had once been so proud. Diabolus, having been publicly disgraced, was bound to the prince's chariot wheels. Then, leaving Captain Boanerges and Captain Conviction on guard at the castle gate, Emmanuel rode triumphantly through the town, out through Eye Gate and on to the plain where his camp lay.

Unless you had been there, you could not imagine the mighty shout that went up from Emmanuel's camp when they saw their beloved prince, with the tyrant tied to his chariot wheels. Then they began to sing, "He has led captivity captive! He has spoiled principalities and powers; Diabolus has been subdued by the power of Emmanuel's sword, and become an object of derision!" Emmanuel then sternly dismissed Diabolus, charging him never to trouble Mansoul again and the tyrant hastily disappeared over the plain, muttering, fuming and raging as he went.

Chapter Eight

A Royal Pardon

The townspeople were now very much taken with the great prince and half hoped that they might not fare too badly at his hand; but they went very much in fear of Captain Boanerges and Captain Conviction, who were still occupying Mr Conscience's house. These were men of great dignity and they, also, like the prince (and at his command) kept their faces set and rather stern. This caused the townspeople to feel great apprehension and suspense, filling them with fears for the future of Mansoul, so that for some time they did not know the meaning of rest or hope or peace of mind.

Emmanuel did not yet dwell in the town, but remained in the royal pavilion in the midst of his camp. He sent special orders to Captain Boanerges to gather the whole of Mansoul into the castle yard and, before them all, to take Lord Willbewill, Lord Understanding and Mr Conscience, and put them in prison under a heavy guard, until the prince should make known his pleasure concerning them. This greatly added to the anxiety of Mansoul, for now they felt that their worst fears were confirmed and they spent all their time wondering what death they would die and how long they would be in dying! For now, to die by the hand of such a good and holy prince seemed a terrible end indeed, although they realised that it was no more than they deserved. They were particularly worried about their three chief men for they felt that, if they were executed, this would surely be the beginning of Mansoul's ruin.

The only thing to do, they felt, was to send another petition to Emmanuel, which they drew up, together with the three men now in prison. The wording was in this form (and, you will notice, a little more urgent than before):

"Great and wonderful lord, victor over Diabolus, and conqueror of Mansoul:

"We, the miserable inhabitants of this now wretched town, do humbly beg that we may find favour in your sight and that you will not remember against us our former sins, nor especially the sins of our chief men. Spare us, according to your great mercy, that we may not die, but live, and become your willing and obedient servants. Amen."

The prince received this second petition, but, again, in complete silence, to the great consternation of the town. Since there was nothing else they could do, they resolved to send yet another petition, with much the same words, by the hand of another messenger, in case the first one had in some way offended the prince. They tried to persuade Captain Conviction to be their messenger, but he would have none of it, saying, "I will not petition Emmanuel on behalf of traitors and rebels! However, our prince is good and noble. If you send by one of your townspeople and he approaches very humbly and pleads for mercy, you may yet succeed where so far you have failed."

They finally decided to send the third petition by the hand of Mr Earnest-Desire, a humble man living in a small cottage near the castle walls, who said he would willingly do anything he could to save the town. Accordingly, they handed the petition to him, with advice on how he should conduct himself before so great a prince, wishing him "good speed" a thousand times over! Arriving at the pavilion he asked for audience with the prince, who came out to see him. As soon as he saw the prince, Mr Earnest-Desire fell on his face to the ground crying, "O, that Mansoul might live before you, O prince!" When Emmanuel read this new petition he was greatly moved and turned aside to weep; but then, addressing Mr Earnest-Desire, who still lay on the ground before him, he said, "Go back to your place and I will consider your request".

As you may imagine, the whole town was eagerly awaiting, though with terrible feelings of guilt and fear, the return of their messenger and they flocked around him to know how he had fared and if Emmanuel had said anything to him. He would tell them nothing, however, until he had come to the prison where the three chief men, Lord Willbe-will, Lord Understanding and Mr Conscience were held. The Lord Mayor was looking as white as a sheet and Mr Conscience was all in a tremble.

"Well," they cried eagerly, "what did the great prince say?"

"When I arrived at the royal pavilion," said Mr Earnest-Desire, "I asked to speak to the prince, who came out to see me; but the majesty and glory of his face made me fall to the ground. As he took the petition from me I cried, 'O, that Mansoul might live before you, O prince!' After reading the contents, he told me to return here and he would consider the request. But O! this prince to whom you sent me is so beautiful and glorious that any who see him are bound both to love and fear him. For my part, I can do no less than that; but what the end of this will be I cannot say."

This news greatly perplexed the three prisoners, as well as the multitude of people listening. They could not think how to interpret the prince's actions and they all ran about the town saying first one thing and then another, but most of them were convinced that the prince's answer meant death for them all. Now, at last, Mansoul was beginning to feel the dreadful effects of its stubbornness and rebellion, being quite overwhelmed with guilt and fear, not least the three chief men who were now prisoners. They decided, in desperation, that they would send yet once more and petition for their lives. This time, the petition was worded much more humbly:

"Prince Emmanuel the great, lord of all worlds and master of mercy, we, your wretched, dying town of Mansoul, do confess to your glorious majesty that we have sinned, both against you and against your great father. We are no more worthy to be called your Mansoul, but are only fit to be cast away for ever. If you kill us, we deserve it. If you condemn us, we cannot but say that you are righteous. We have no ground to complain, whatever you think fit to do. But O! let your mercy be extended to us; let it free us from our sin and guilt and we will for ever sing of your mercy and judgement. Amen."

The question now was, "who should take this petition?" Someone suggested Mr Good-Deed for a messenger, but Mr Conscience opposed this very strongly.

"How," he argued, "can we send our petition for mercy

by a man with such a name? If the prince should ask him his name, as he may well do, and he replies 'Old Mr Good-Deed', will not Emmanuel say, 'Is old Good-Deed yet alive in Mansoul? Then let old Good-Deed save you in your trouble'. And if he says that, then we are certainly lost, for a thousand Good-Deeds could not save Mansoul now."

The Recorder pressed his point so strongly that those who had, at first, been in favour of sending Mr Good-Deed, were easily persuaded to put him on one side and it was finally decided to send Mr Earnest-Desire again, who asked if he might this time be accompanied by his poor and lowly friend Mr Tearful. (This Mr Tearful, the son of Mr Repentance, was a man very broken in spirit, but one who could well present a petition for mercy.) They were both urged to be particularly careful in their words and conduct, for it was felt that a mistake at this crucial point could well result in the total destruction of Mansoul.

Arriving at the royal pavilion, they were rather worried in case their continual coming might be regarded by the prince as a nuisance; so they first made their apology, saying that they had no wish to be troublesome, but necessity demanded that they should come again. They added that they could not rest, day or night, because of their transgressions against Emmanuel and El Shaddai. Having said this, they both fell down at the prince's feet, Mr Earnest-Desire crying as before, "O, that Mansoul might live before you, O prince!"

The prince, having read the petition, came to the two petitioners and, telling them to rise to their feet, he spoke to them as they stood trembling before him.

"Mansoul has grievously rebelled against my father, in rejecting him from being its king and choosing instead a liar and a murderer. As for Diabolus, your pretended prince, he has already rebelled in the highest court and been cast out. When my father sent a powerful army to bring you to obedience, you resisted his captains, shutting your gates and fighting against them with that evil Diabolus. Then, when my father sent me, did you cry for mercy? As long as there was any hope that you might prevail you stubbornly resisted, turning a deaf ear to all my offers. But, now that I have taken the town, you cry! Why did you not call upon me when the white flag of mercy, the red flag of justice and the black flag of threatened execution were flown? Now that I have conquered your Diabolus, you come to me for favour; but why did you not help me against my enemy?

"However, I will consider your petition and answer in a way that will be for my glory. Tell Captain Boanerges and Captain Conviction to bring the three chief prisoners out to me in the camp tomorrow; at the same time tell Captain Judgement and Captain Execution to stay in the castle and keep all quiet in Mansoul until they hear further from me."

With this, the prince turned on his heel and went back into his royal pavilion.

Mr Earnest-Desire and Mr Tearful returned quickly to Mansoul, where the townsmen were once again eagerly awaiting their arrival and they all hurried together to the chief prisoners. There they related how Emmanuel had reminded them that they had not only chosen to fight with Diabolus, but had despised the prince and his men. (At this, the prisoners turned even paler than they were already.) They concluded by saying that the prince intended to consider their petition and would do what was most for his glory. Mr Tearful then gave some very heavy sighs and they were all cast right "down in the dumps", but even more so, when a Mr Inquisitive asked if there was nothing else.

"Well, yes," was their reluctant answer, "the prince also said that we were to tell Captain Boanerges and Captain

Conviction to bring the prisoners to him in his camp tomorrow, while Captain Judgement and Captain Execution take care of the town until they hear further from him. When he had said this, he turned his back upon us and went into his royal pavilion."

This last piece of news was terrible indeed and Lord Willbewill, Lord Understanding and Mr Conscience each prepared himself to die.

"This is what I have feared all along," said old Mr Conscience sadly. The whole town, feeling that this would also be their fate sooner or later, spent the night in mourning.

Next day, when the time was come, all the townspeople, dressed in black, stood upon the walls, hoping by this to move the heart of the prince in pity toward them. The prisoners had also dressed themselves in black clothes, putting ropes around their necks, and they were then led out of the city in chains. Captain Boanerges went in front, with a guard, and Captain Conviction came behind; the soldiers went with flying colours, but the prisoners went with drooping spirits.

Reaching the door of the royal pavilion, they were taken before the prince, who was seated upon his throne of state. They immediately cast themselves, trembling, on the ground before him, hiding their faces for very shame. The prince commanded them to stand for questioning:

Emmanuel: "Are you the men who were once the servants of El Shaddai?"

Prisoners: "Yes, lord, yes."

Emmanuel: "Are you the men who allowed yourselves to be corrupted and defiled by the abominable Diabolus?"

Prisoners: "We did more than allow it, lord. We chose it for ourselves."

Emmanuel: "Could you have been content to live under his slavery for ever?"

Prisoners: "Yes, lord, yes; for his ways were very pleasing to our flesh and we no longer desired anything better."

Emmanuel: "And when I came up against the town of Mansoul, did you not heartily wish that I might *not* be victorious?"

Prisoners: "Yes, lord, indeed we did."

Emmanuel: "And what punishment do you think you deserve at my hand for these and all your other grievous transgressions?"

Prisoners: "We deserve nothing but death and destruction, lord."

Emmanuel: "Have you anything to suggest, why this punishment which you deserve should not be passed upon you?"

Prisoners: "We can say nothing, lord. You are just – and we have sinned."

Emmanuel: "And what are those ropes around your necks?"

Prisoners: "To bind us to the place of execution, if mercy is not granted to us."

Emmanuel: "Are all the men of Mansoul included in your confession?"

Prisoners: "All the natives of the town are included, my lord; but we cannot answer for the Diabolonians who are still there."

At this, the prince commanded that a herald should proclaim throughout the camp that Emmanuel had, in his father's name and for his father's glory, gained a complete victory over Mansoul. The prisoners were to follow the herald saying "Amen". This was done exactly as the prince ordered. The captains shouted, the soldiers sang songs of triumph to their prince, the colours waved in the wind and there was great joy everywhere – but not yet in the hearts of the men of Mansoul.

The prince called for the prisoners to be brought before him again and once more they stood trembling in his presence. He then addressed them in this amazing manner:

"The sins, trespasses and iniquities which you, with the whole town of Mansoul, have committed against my father and against me, I have power and commandment to forgive . . . and I hereby forgive you accordingly."

Having said this, he handed to them, written on parchment and sealed with seven great seals, a large and general pardon, to be proclaimed by the Lord Mayor, Lord Willbewill and Mr Conscience throughout the town of Mansoul at sunrise on the following day.

After this, the prince himself stripped off their black clothing, giving them instead "beauty for ashes, the oil of joy for mourning, and the garment of praise for the spirit of heaviness". He then gave to each of the three men jewels of gold and precious stones, taking away their ropes and putting chains of gold about their necks and earrings in their ears.

When the prisoners heard the gracious words of the prince and saw all that was done to them, they almost fainted away! For the grace, the pardon, was so tremendous, so glorious, so utterly unexpected, that they could hardly stand up under it. In fact, Lord Willbewill staggered and would have fallen, but the prince stepped quickly to him and, putting his arms under him, embraced and kissed him, assuring him that all should be fulfilled according to his words. He also kissed and embraced the other two men and, smiling upon them, said, "Take these gifts as tokens of my love, favour and compassion toward you. And be sure to tell in Mansoul all that you have seen and heard".

Then their chains were broken in pieces and they each fell down before the prince, kissing his feet and wetting them with their tears, crying aloud, in their relief, "Blessed be the glory of the lord from this place".

They were then told to arise and go back to tell Mansoul all that the prince had done. A piper went before them and Captain Faith, with some of his senior officers, was ordered to march before these noblemen into the town. Captain Faith was also commanded that, when Mr Conscience began to read the pardon in the town, he should, at that very moment, march in at Eye Gate with colours flying and, with all his men in attendance, go straight up to Heart Castle. Here he should take possession until the prince himself should come, telling Captain Judgement and Captain Execution to leave the stronghold, withdraw from Mansoul and return immediately to the camp. (For know this, that when faith and pardon meet together, judgement and execution depart from the heart!) In this way, Mansoul was delivered from the terror of the first four captains and their men.

Chapter Nine

Emmanuel's Triumphant Entry

While all these wonderful things were happening the townspeople were waiting, with great sadness of heart, expecting at any moment to hear of the death of their three chief men. They kept looking anxiously over the walls, until at last they thought they saw someone approaching. Can you begin to imagine their amazement when they saw the prisoners returning, and with such splendour and honour? They had gone down to the camp clad in black, yet they returned in beautiful garments! They had gone with ropes around their necks; they came back with chains of gold! They had gone expecting death, yet they came back with the assurance of life! They had gone with heavy, drooping spirits and they came back accompanied by pipes and joyful music!

As they approached Eye Gate, the poor, tottering town of Mansoul gave such a shout, that it made the captains and the prince's army jump with surprise! – and who could blame them? It was like life from the dead to see their friends coming back in such splendour. They greeted each other with, "Welcome, welcome. Blessed is he that spared you. We see that it is well with you but how is it to fare with the town of Mansoul? Will it be well for us also?"

Then Mr Conscience and the Lord Mayor cried aloud, "O! tidings! glad tidings! good tidings of great joy to poor Mansoul!"

Another great shout of joy arose from the town and then the three former prisoners related all that had taken place in the camp, while the people wondered greatly at the wisdom and grace of the Prince Emmanuel.

Mr Conscience declared, "For all Mansoul there is pardon! pardon! pardon! And this you shall hear in full tomorrow!"

He then commanded that, in the morning, all the town should gather together in the market-place, to hear their general pardon declared to them.

It is almost impossible to describe the change this effected in Mansoul. No man could sleep that night for joy and from every house came the sound of music and singing, rejoicing and gladness.

"O!" they cried to each other, "we shall hear more of this at day-break tomorrow. Who could have thought, yesterday, that *this* day would be such a day of rejoicing? Who would have expected to see our prisoners returning in chains of gold? Is this the common custom of princes? Do they usually show such favour to traitors? No, such grace is peculiar to Emmanuel and El Shaddai alone! Truly they have not dealt with us as we deserve, nor rewarded us according to our sins."

At sunrise on the following morning, Mr Conscience, Lord Understanding and Lord Willbewill came down to the market-place at the time appointed by the prince, where all the townsfolk were already assembled, waiting for them. They came still dressed in the glory with which the prince had adorned them the previous day. The multitude of eager, hopeful people then accompanied them to Mouth Gate, which is at the lower end of the market-place, for this is where all public matters were read and declared.

After beckoning for silence, Mr Conscience read out the pardon in a loud, clear voice; but when he came to these words, "The lord, the lord God, merciful and gracious, pardoning iniquity, transgressions, and sins; and to them all manner of sin and blasphemy shall be forgiven . . ." the listening people could keep silent no longer and they leapt and shouted for joy, because every man's name was adjoined to that glorious pardon! At the same time, the silver trumpets sounded forth from Emmanuel's camp to show that all his men also were rejoicing in the grace and mercy that had been shown to Mansoul by their prince. Nor could Captain Faith keep silent, but joined in with trumpets from the battlements of the castle.

When the reading was ended, the townsmen ran upon the walls of the town, still leaping and shouting; they bowed themselves seven times, with their faces towards Emmanuel's pavilion, calling forth, "Let Emmanuel live for ever!" Then all the young men were commanded to ring the bells throughout the town, while the people sang and, once again, there was music in every part of Mansoul.

Very little time elapsed before the whole town went forth to thank the prince, to praise him for his wonderful favour to them and to beg that he would be pleased to come into Mansoul, with all his men, and dwell among them. In deep humility the leading men bowed before the prince, who greeted them with, "My peace be upon you". At this they drew near to touch the top of his golden sceptre and told him of their desire.

"We have ample room for you, O prince, and all your men, if you will come and dwell in our town, for we desire you to be king of Mansoul for ever. Govern us according to all your wishes and we will gladly be your obedient and loyal servants. For indeed," they added, having presented their request, "if you and your captains should now withdraw, O gracious Emmanuel, after all the benefits and mercies you have bestowed upon this miserable town, Mansoul will surely die. For our enemies will come upon us again, with even greater rage and spite than before. We beseech you to grant our request, for you are truly the desire of our eyes and the life and strength of this town. There may well be Diabolonians still hiding amongst us, who will plot and betray us again into the hands of Diabolus, and we dread the very thought of falling into his terrible clutches again. O, let it please your grace to accept Heart Castle for his royal residence."

To this, Emmanuel replied, "If I come to dwell in your town, will you allow me to do all that is in my heart toward my enemies and yours? Will you, in fact, help me in such an undertaking?"

"O Prince Emmanuel," was their pitiful reply, "we do not know what we shall do. We did not think, once, that we could ever have been traitors to El Shaddai, as we have proved to be. What can we say to you, O lord? We dare not promise anything. Come and dwell amongst us and make us safe; conquer us with your love and your grace; set your noble captains as governors over us; then surely we shall comply with your wishes and gladly fulfil your will. One word more we would add. We know so little of your wisdom, O our gracious prince. How could we have ever imagined that so much sweetness and joy could have issued out of our bitter trials? But if *you* will take us by the hand and lead us by your wise counsels, then all things will be for the best for your Mansoul. O lord, come to your Mansoul, do what you will, only keep us from sinning and make us serviceable to your majesty."

The prince smiled tenderly as he listened to this humble and affecting plea and replied, "Go, return to your houses in peace and I will gladly comply with your desire. To-morrow, I will remove my royal pavilion and I will march through Eye Gate, with all my forces, into the town of Mansoul. I will possess myself of your castle and I will set my captains and soldiers over you. Indeed, I will yet do things in Mansoul that cannot find their equal under the whole heaven."

The townsmen hereupon gave another great shout of gladness and delight and returned to their houses, telling their relatives and friends of the good that Emmanuel had promised to Mansoul. Upon hearing this, all the people went with haste to the trees and the meadows to gather great armfuls of branches and flowers, with which to strew the streets along which their prince would pass from Eye Gate right up to the gate of Heart Castle.

On the next day the gates were flung wide open and the nobles and elders of Mansoul waited to greet Emmanuel with a thousand welcomes. O! what a glorious sight was seen that day, as the prince entered the town through Eye Gate, clad in his golden armour and riding in his royal chariot, with the trumpets sounding before him, the colours of his captains waving gloriously in the wind and his thousands of men in attendance. Everyone was eager to behold the triumphal entry of the prince, the windows and balconies, yes, even the roof-tops being filled with waving, rejoicing people, singing to each other, "Surely he is the fairest of ten thousand and the altogether lovely one!" Captain Faith came out of the castle to conduct Emmanuel into his new residence which he had been preparing for him; and so, this royal prince of princes came at last to dwell in his redeemed Mansoul!

It seemed, now, that the elders of the town just could not have enough of Emmanuel, his person, his words, his actions, everything about him being so pleasing and desirable to them. They begged, therefore, that although Heart Castle was his residence, he would very often visit the streets and the houses and the people of the town. "For, great sovereign," they said, "your looks and smiles and words are now the very life and light of Mansoul."

They requested that they might have continued access to him, without difficulty or interruption, and for this purpose he commanded that the castle gate should always stand open. Whenever he spoke, they all listened most carefully, and began to imitate him in his speech and ways.

One day, Emmanuel made a feast for the whole town and everyone came to the castle for the banquet. He feasted them with all kinds of foods that were strange to them, which had been brought especially from his father's court. Dish after dish[1] was set before them and they were encouraged to eat freely; and although, when a new dish was set before them, they often whispered to each other, "What is it?", yet they ate and enjoyed it, and drank deeply of the water that had been turned into wine. When the feasting was over, Emmanuel, to entertain his guests, asked

[1] Promise after promise.

them many curious riddles of secrets drawn up by his father's secretary, and by the wisdom and skill of El Shaddai. They were all to do with the great king, or his son Emmanuel, and about his wars and doings with Mansoul. Emmanuel explained some of them to the people, who were both enlightened and amazed that such wisdom could be expressed in so few words. As they went home from the banquet, they could not stop talking of the wonderful things that had been explained to them and they talked and sang about their prince in their homes and some even sang of him in their sleep!

Emmanuel had decided that he would remodel this town that he loved until it was most pleasing to himself, ensuring that it would be quite safe from any future trouble that might arise either within or without the gates. To accomplish this, he ordered that all the golden slings which had come from his father's court should be mounted upon towers and battlements, to defend the town against any further enemies that might try to attack. Then he called Lord Willbewill and put him in charge of the gates, the walls and the towers, charging him that, if he should find any Diabolonians lurking in the town, he should capture them immediately and keep them in safe custody. After this, he called Lord Understanding, the original Lord Mayor, and reinstated him in that office (and in it he remained for the rest of his life). He was told to read continually in the revelation of mysteries,[1] so that he could perform his work rightly. Mr Knowledge was appointed to the position of Recorder; this was not to put any slight upon Mr Conscience, but because it was in the prince's mind to confer another position upon him, of which you will hear eventually. The image of Diabolus was taken down at the prince's command, beaten into powder and cast to the

[1] The Bible.

four winds outside the walls of the town, after which the image of El Shaddai was set up again, together with the image of the prince, upon the castle gates, and his name, "Emmanuel", engraved in gold on the wall at the front of the town. Yet all this was but the beginning of the good prince's loving plans for the welfare and honour of his Mansoul.

Chapter Ten

The Trial of the Diabolonians

The time had now come for the trial of the three chief Diabolonians and several others who had been captured by the now brave and valiant Lord Willbewill. These were the two late Lord Mayors, Lord Evil-Desire and Lord Unbelief, with the Recorder Mr Forget-Good; in addition there were such men as Alderman Atheism, Alderman Hard-Heart and Alderman False-Peace, with Mr No-Truth, Mr Haughty and Mr Pitiless. It would take me too long to give you an account of each of these trials, so I will just recount one or two, or perhaps three, as samples of them all.

When the court was set Mr True-Man, the jailor, was commanded to bring his prisoners to the bar, so in they came, all chained together. When they had been presented before the Lord Mayor, the Recorder (now Mr Knowledge) and the rest of the honourable bench, the jury and the witnesses were sworn in. The jury was composed of twelve good, honest men, bearing the names Mr Belief, Mr True-Heart, Mr Upright, Mr Hate-Bad, Mr Love-God, Mr See-Truth, Mr Heavenly-Mind, Mr Moderate, Mr Good-Work, Mr Zeal-for-God, Mr Thankful and Mr Humble. The witnesses were Mr Know-Well, Mr Tell-True and Mr Hate-Lies.

Some of the trials were quite long and involved, but that of Unbelief was quickly settled. Being brought to the bar, he was charged in the following manner:

Clerk: "Lord Unbelief, you are here indicted under this name of Unbelief (which shows you to be not a native, but an intruder in this town) because, when you were an officer in Mansoul, you did most wickedly stand out against the captains of El Shaddai. You roused the town to a state of great defiance against the name, the army and the cause of the great king and, together with your evil master Diabolus, you encouraged the townspeople unceasingly to resist their true and lawful king. What have you to say to this charge? Are you guilty, or not guilty?"

Unbelief: "I say that I do not know El Shaddai. I love my old master, Diabolus, and I thought it my duty to be true to him and to possess the minds of the men of Mansoul so that they would resist to their utmost any strangers and foreigners. I have *not* changed my opinion, nor do I intend to change it, even though I am at present under the power of this court."

Then said the court, "This man, as all can see, is quite unrepentant, and will maintain his wickedness unmoved. Set him by, jailor, and call the next prisoner."

Upon this, Mr Atheism was called to the bar; a comparatively young man, with a scornful face.

Clerk: "Mr Atheism, you are here indicted under that name (which shows you at once to be an intruder in this town) because you have persistently and deliberately taught and maintained that there is no God and therefore no one has any need to be religious. This you have done against the being, honour and glory of the great king and against the peace and safety of Mansoul. What have you to say? Are you guilty, or not guilty?"

Atheism: "Not guilty, my lord."

Crier: "Call Mr Know-Well, Mr Tell-True and Mr Hate-Lies into the court."

(These men were called and appeared immediately.)

Clerk: "You, the witnesses for the king, look upon the prisoner at the bar and say whether you know him."

Mr Know-Well: "Yes, my lord, we know him. His name is Atheism and he has been a cause of mischief in this town far too long."

Clerk: "You are sure that you know him?"

Mr Know-Well: "Know him? Yes, indeed, my lord, I know him well. I have too often been in his company to be ignorant of him. He is a Diabolonian, and the son of a Diabolonian! I knew both his father and his grandfather intimately also."

Clerk: "Very well. He is charged with teaching and maintaining that there is no God and so no need for anyone to be religious. What do you say to this, you three witnesses?"

Mr Know-Well: "Once, when I was walking with him, I heard him say that although he did not believe there was a God, yet he could quite easily profess to believe and be as religious as any, if the company he was in, or the circumstances of the moment, required it. Upon my oath I have heard him say this."

Clerk: "Mr Tell-True, have you anything to say to the king's judges concerning this prisoner?"

Mr Tell-True: "My lord, I was once a close friend of this man Atheism (I blush to confess it) and I have often heard him say, most emphatically, that he believed in neither God, angel, nor spirit. He is a man who delights to speak blasphemous and horrible things against the living God. I know him to be the son of a Diabolonian, for his father's name was Never-be-Good. I have nothing more to say."

Clerk: "Mr Hate-Lies, look upon this prisoner at the bar and tell me if you know him."

Mr Hate-Lies: "Indeed I do, my lord. I know him to be one of the vilest men that I have ever had to do with. I have heard him declare openly that there is no God, no world to come, no sin, and no punishment hereafter and that he would far rather go to a place of sin than endure listening to a sermon."

Mr Atheism was accordingly set on one side and Mr No-Truth called to the bar.

Clerk: "Mr No-Truth, you are here indicted by this name (which reveals you also as an intruder into this town) and you are charged with spitefully defacing the image of El Shaddai, also of utterly destroying every trace of his good laws, to the ruin of this town of Mansoul after it had rebelled against its rightful king. What do you say? Are you guilty, or not guilty?"

Mr No-Truth: "Not guilty, my lord."

Hereupon the first witness, Mr Know-Well, was called to give his evidence.

Mr Know-Well: "My lord, this man was at the pulling down of the image of El Shaddai, for I stood by and saw him do it with his own hands, at the command of Diabolus. He also set up the hideous image of his evil master in its place and did tear and destroy and cause to be consumed every trace that he could find of the laws of the great king."

Clerk: "Did anyone else see him do this beside yourself?"

Here Mr Hate-Lies stepped forward to give his evidence.

Mr Hate-Lies: "I saw him, my lord, and so did many others, for this thing was not done by stealth, but in open view of all. Indeed, he chose to do it publicly, for he took great delight and pleasure in his evil actions."

Clerk: "Mr No-Truth, how could you brazenly declare yourself not guilty, when you were so undisputedly the doer of this wickedness?"

Mr No-Truth: "Well, sir, I had to say something and I always speak true to my name. It has often served me well in the past, never to speak the truth, and I hoped it might advantage me now."

All the trials proceeded in a manner similar to these three, and when every case had been brought before the court, the jury were asked to withdraw and carefully consider what verdict they could bring in, to uphold the cause of truth and righteousness for their king, within the town of Mansoul. The twelve men, therefore, withdrew to discuss the cases amongst themselves and you will notice that their comments were remarkably true to their individual name and character.

Mr Belief: (He was the foreman). "Gentlemen, for my part, I am convinced that all these prisoners are only worthy of death."

Mr True-Heart: "Very true. I am whole-heartedly of your opinion."

Mr Hate-Bad: "O what a mercy it is that such villains as these have been captured at last."

Mr Love-God: "Yes. Yes. This is certainly one of the most joyful days of my whole life."

Mr See-Truth: "I am certain if we say that these men should die, our verdict will stand before El Shaddai himself."

Mr Heavenly-Mind: "I do not question that. When all such beastly characters as these are cast out, what a lovely place Mansoul will be."

Mr Moderate: "As you know, it is never my manner to pass judgement rashly, but, for crimes such as we have listened to, vouched for by such reliable witnesses, I think the man must be wilfully blind who could say that such men should not die."

Mr Thankful: "O, how I thank and bless God that these traitors are now held in safe custody."

Mr Humble: "I would join you, on my bare knees, in thanking God for delivering Mansoul from these rogues."

Mr Good-Work: "It will be a pleasure to see these men receive a fit reward for all their evil conduct in this town."

Mr Zeal-for-God: "Let them be cut off, and that without delay, for they have already done harm enough amongst us."

The jury then returned to the court and the foreman, Mr Belief, told the judge that a verdict of "Guilty" had been passed upon every prisoner. Upon this, sentence was passed by the judge, and the jailor led his prisoners away, locking them all in the safest part of the prison until the time of the execution, which was to be the following morning. But by some means (no-one knows how) that crafty old Unbelief managed to break from prison and make his escape right out of the town, where he remained lurking about, hoping that he might yet be able to do some damage to Mansoul, in revenge for the way in which he had been treated. When the jailor, Mr True-Man, discovered that he had lost this prisoner, he was very troubled, for old Unbelief was really the worst of them all. He quickly reported the escape to the Lord Mayor, Lord Willbewill, and the Recorder, but although they instantly organised a most thorough search, not a trace of Unbelief could be found anywhere in the town of Mansoul!

In actual fact, Unbelief roamed and searched until he found his old master Diabolus and then what a story he had to tell of all that Emmanuel had done in Mansoul.

"Not only has this prince given the town a general pardon (can you credit that?) but he has taken up residence in the castle," bemoaned Unbelief, "with his soldiers quite filling the town. Worst of all, they have pulled down your image, O my master, at the command of the prince, and set up his image and that of his father again. As if this were not enough, that wretched Willbewill is now in as great favour with Emmanuel as he once was with you. He has captured eight of your most trusty servants, who have been publicly tried and condemned to death; no doubt they have been executed by now and such would have been my fate also, had I not craftily managed to escape."

How Diabolus stamped with rage when he heard this story! He fumed and yelled, as he breathed out threatenings, vowing that he would yet be revenged upon Mansoul. Finally, he and Unbelief promised each other that they would plot together and see how they might get into the town again.

Meanwhile, when the time of execution drew near, Mansoul very solemnly brought the condemned men to the cross; for the prince had said that he wished this act to be performed by the hands of the townsmen themselves, as a proof of their sincerity, and to see how ready they now were to obey his word and do his pleasure. The townsmen then took hold of these evil Diabolonians to kill them, but what a troublesome task this proved to be! The prisoners struggled and twisted and squirmed, until the men of Mansoul had to cry out for help, which came to them from Emmanuel's secretary who was in the town. He was a great lover of Mansoul, and was at the place of execution. Hearing their urgent cries for help against the struggling and resisting Diabolonians, he came to their aid, putting his strong hand upon the hands of the townsmen and so these evil men, who had been such a plague and grief to the town, were crucified at last.

Chapter Eleven

The Joy of Emmanuel's Presence

The prince was very pleased with the obedience of his Mansoul in the matter of dealing with these Diabolonians and came down to see them and speak comfortingly to them. He said that as they had now proved by this act the reality of their love to him and their respect for his commandments, he intended to honour them with another captain, whom he had chosen from amongst themselves. Calling a servant to him, he said, "Go immediately to the castle gate. Enquire there for Mr Experience, who is serving under Captain Faith, and tell him to come to me here, without delay." Mr Experience came quickly in response to this summons and bowed low before his prince. The townsmen knew Mr Experience well, for he was born and bred in Mansoul and, although still quite a young man, was both brave and wise, a man who was careful in his conduct, well-spoken, and pleasant in his person. The hearts of the people were overjoyed, therefore, when they saw that the prince obviously thought very highly of Mr Experience and intended to make him a captain amongst them.

"Young man," said the prince, "I am putting you in a position of trust and honour in this my dear town of Mansoul. You shall be captain over a thousand men."

Upon hearing of his unexpected promotion, Mr Experience bowed his head and worshipped, while the people shouted, "Let Emmanuel live for ever! Let our great prince live for ever!"

A commission was immediately drawn up for him by the Lord Secretary and sealed with Emmanuel's own seal. As soon as the new captain had received his commission, he sounded his trumpet for volunteers, and from all over Mansoul young men came hastening to serve under him, including sons of the great and chief men of the town. Mr Skilful and Mr Memory served as officers under him; his colours were the white colours of the town and his coat-of-arms showed a dead bear and a dead lion. Then the elders of the town came to thank the prince for his love, care and tender compassion to the town of Mansoul and they all enjoyed sweet fellowship together.

It was at this time, also, that Emmanuel decided to renew and amend the town's charter. This he did, not because the people asked him to, but because it was ever the habit of this good prince to be thinking of new ways in which to add to his people's welfare and happiness. Having examined the old charter, he put it on one side, saying that old things had now passed away and he was making all things new. Here is a summary of its contents, although this was not all of it by any means:

"Emmanuel, prince of peace and a great lover of Mansoul.

I do, in the name of my father and of my own mercy, give, grant and bequeath to my beloved town of Mansoul free, full and everlasting forgiveness of all wrongs, injuries and offences done by them against my father, against me, against their neighbours or themselves.

I do give them the holy law and my covenant and all that it contains, for their everlasting comfort and consolation.

I do also give them a portion of the self-same grace and goodness that dwells in my father's heart and mine.

I do give, grant and bestow upon them the world and all that is in it, for their good. I grant them the benefits of life and death, of things present and things to come.

I do give and grant them leave and free access to me in my palace at all seasons (that is, to my palace above or below), there to make known their wants to me; and I give them my promise to hear and redress all their grievances.

I do give, grant to, and invest the town of Mansoul with full power and authority to seek out and destroy all manner of Diabolonians that may be found at any time in or near Mansoul.

I do further grant authority not to allow any stranger or foreigner to share in the grants and privileges of this town, but that they shall be solely for true inhabitants and their descendants."

This gracious charter, being given to the town from the hand of the prince, was immediately carried to Mouth Gate, in the market-place, where Mr Knowledge read it in the presence of all the people. It was then taken back to Heart Castle and engraved upon the doors in letters of gold so that the town of Mansoul might have it always in view. Thus, being continually reminded of the blessed freedom and privileges bestowed upon them by their prince, their joy would be increased and also their love renewed and strengthened toward their great and good Emmanuel.

What joy now possessed the town as the bells rang again and again, the minstrels played, the people danced and sang, and the silver trumpets sounded forth all over the town. (The remaining Diabolonians in the town, I might tell you, were thankful to hide their heads quite out of sight and hope to be overlooked and forgotten.)

Soon after this the prince sent for the elders and chiefs of the town, informing them that he intended to establish a new ministry in Mansoul. "For," he said, "unless you have teachers and guides, you will not be able to know and do my father's will."

When the elders told this news to the people they all came running to hear more of this (for now, whatever pleased the prince pleased the people!), and they begged him to establish such a ministry amongst them.

He told them that there were to be two preachers, one from his father's court and one chosen from among the men of the town.

"He that is from my father's court is of no less dignity and quality than my father and I. He is the Lord Chief Secretary of my father's court, the one who dictates all my father's laws and who understands all mysteries and knowledge, just as my father and I do. He is, in fact, one with us in nature and he has as great a love and concern for Mansoul as we have and will be your chief teacher in all things. Take care that you do not grieve him, but rather love and obey him. He is the only one, apart from myself, who knows the ways and methods of my father's court: nor does anyone know, as he does, all that is in the heart of my father toward Mansoul. He, alone, can tell Mansoul what to do to keep in my father's love and he can bring forgotten things back to your remembrance again.

"His personal dignity, the excellence of his teaching and his willingness to help you in all matters must cause you to love, obey and fear him continually. He must help you to frame all the petitions that you present to my father and, without his advice and counsel, let nothing enter into either the town or the castle, lest you disgust and grieve this noble person; for then he might turn and fight against you. But, if you obey and love him, if you devote yourself to his teaching, if you keep in continual fellowship with him, you will find that he is ten times more to you than the whole world itself. Listen to him, therefore; love him and heed his teaching, for he alone can shed abroad the love of my father in your hearts. So will my Mansoul be the wisest and most blessed of people."

The prince then called old Mr Conscience to him, telling him that as he was well-skilled in the law and government of the town, he was appointed to be the other minister, but always *under* the Lord Secretary. He was warned to keep to his own sphere and never to presume to teach the higher and spiritual matters which only the Lord Secretary could teach and interpret.

"Wherefore, O Mr Conscience," warned the prince, "always be ready to learn and be taught by him yourself; always keep yourself low and humble before him.

"But now", added the prince addressing the townsmen again, "I must give you a word of solemn warning. I know well, as you will also know before very long, that there are still Diabolonians lurking within your walls who are sturdy and implacable enemies. They will not hesitate to plot against you, even though I am in your midst, in the hope of bringing you again into bondage, for they are the sworn friends of Diabolus. So beware! You must be very diligent in hunting them out, putting them immediately to death and you must not heed *any* terms of peace which they may offer you. So that you may easily recognise them, the names of their chief men are Lord Murder, Lord Adultery, Lord Anger, Lord Deceit, Mr Revelling, Mr Witchcraft, Mr Strife, Mr Wrath, Mr Envy, Mr Heresy and the like. If you look carefully into the laws of the king, you will find them clearly described and you will detect them more easily. I warn you that these very men are now skulking within your town and if you leave them alone they will poison your captains and weaken your soldiers, turning your now flourishing Mansoul into a desolate wilderness.

"I confirm that I have given you full permission and power to seek out and to put to death by crucifixion any Diabolonians who at any time may be found within or around the walls of your town. Wherefore, O my Mansoul, watch and be sober, and do not let yourself be betrayed by your own carelessness."

Still the prince's kind and loving thoughts for the town were not exhausted, for on another day he called all the people to his palace and provided every person with a white and glistening garment, brought out of his treasury, so that they were all, without exception, clothed in fine linen, clean and white.

"This is my badge of honour," explained the prince, "which marks you as my servants and separates you from all other people, for no-one else can give such clothing as this. Wear these garments always, to show your love for your prince, that all the world may know that you are mine."

"Here are my instructions regarding your clothes," he continued. "Wear them daily, so that you will always appear to be my people. Keep them always white, for if they are soiled my name is dishonoured. Do not let them drag in the dust of the earth. Take care that you do not lose them for this will be for your shame. But, if you *should* defile them (I hope you will not, although Diabolus will be pleased if you do), then seek immediately to do what is in my law and put right whatever you have done wrong.

"This is the way to ensure that I will never leave you nor forsake you, O my Mansoul."

Now Mansoul was glorious indeed! Where could be found a town to compare with it, a town redeemed from the hand and power of Diabolus, a town loved by King Shaddai and for whose deliverance he had even sent his well-beloved son, a town in which the lovely Emmanuel delighted to dwell? Mansoul, once so degraded and filthy, now had a most excellent prince, glittering captains and men of war, and a people robed in garments as white as snow.

When all the remodelling of the town was complete, the prince's own royal standard, the great golden flag, was flown from the battlements of the castle. To show his delight in the town, he gave them many visits. Not a day passed without either the elders coming to him, or he to them, when they would walk and talk together of the great things which Emmanuel had already done, or proposed to do, in his town. These joys, however, were not only for the elders. How graciously and tenderly did this noble prince behave towards the ordinary folk of the town; and how they loved him! Wherever he went, in the streets, houses or gardens, he brought blessing with him! If any were ill, he would lay his hands upon them and heal them. He would also encourage his captains with his smiles and his presence—for, you must know, that one smile from him could put more life and vigour into them than anything else under heaven.

Hardly a week went by but he gave a feast for his people and never did he send them away empty handed, but always with a ring, or a gold chain, or some other token of his love and favour. If the people did not visit him as frequently as he wished, he would himself go and knock at their doors, making sure that their love towards him was unchanged.

How amazing it was that, in the very place where Diabolus had once had his abode, entertaining his Diabolonians almost to the destruction of Mansoul, the prince of princes should now sit, eating and drinking with his redeemed people, his captains and his men, in sweet and pure and loving fellowship. Now might Mansoul well say, "How great is his goodness; for since I have found favour in his sight, how honourable have I been."

The prince now set, as governor over the whole of the town, a great gentleman from his father's court named Mr God's-Peace. (He was under the Lord Secretary, of course, but over all the inhabitants of the town and there were some who were sure that he was related to Captain Faith and Captain Good-Hope.) It was noticeable that, as long as all things in Mansoul were arranged as this sweet-natured gentleman desired, the town was in the most happy condition. There was no arguing or quarrelling or bickering, no unfaithfulness or interfering. Each man kept to his own position, while the women and children would work and sing, work and sing, from morning till night. In the whole of the town, nothing could be found but harmony, quietness, joy and health; and this lasted throughout the whole of that delightful summer.

Mansoul—a redeemed and happy people

PART TWO

BACK-SLIDING AND RESTORATION

Chapter Twelve

Where, O Where is Emmanuel?

Now very sadly I must tell you this. Within the town of Mansoul there lived a man called Mr False-Security and he was a Diabolonian. (His father was a Mr Self-Conceit who had come into the town when Diabolus first took possession. Because of his boldness and daring, he had been set in office next to Lord Willbewill.) When Emmanuel was attacking the town, this man had been one of the loudest in urging the people to resist and defy the prince; but when he saw that the prince was likely to be the victor and then saw Diabolus driven out of his nest and publicly disgraced, he changed sides as easily as blinking an eye-lid. He began to mingle with the townspeople, becoming quite popular with them, for he knew well how to say the right things at just the right time.

Realising that the town was now strong and powerful, he began to praise up the fortifications and the great captains, knowing that this would be well received by the people and increase his popularity amongst them. He took care repeatedly to emphasise the prince's assurance that Mansoul would now be happy for ever. Gradually, by his wily talking, he drew the people after him and they soon began to feel more and more secure. They turned from talking to feasting, then from feasting to sporting, relaxing into careless ways as the days passed by. (All this time, Emmanuel was in the town and he wisely observed what was taking place.) The Lord Mayor, Lord Willbewill and Mr Knowledge (the new Recorder) were greatly taken up with this man, forgetting that their good prince had warned them to be on their guard against disguised Diabolonians. He had warned them also that the security of the now flourishing town did not really lie in their fortifications or possessions, but rather in so keeping his will that he would always dwell in Heart Castle. *He* was their strength and *his presence* was their salvation. It was by continuing steadfastly and obediently in his love and in his father's love that they would be strong. Therefore, they should have heard their prince, feared their prince, loved their prince and obeyed him by stoning this evil man to death – not falling in love with him and letting him lead them where he would.

When the blessed Emmanuel saw that this Diabolonian had caused the townsmen's love to be chilled toward him, he first sadly spoke of their state to the Lord Secretary, saying, "O that my people had paid attention to me and walked in my ways. For then would their peace have been as a river and their righteousness as the waves of the sea. Have I been such a wilderness to them that my people have forgotten me days without number?" He then said, "I will return to my father's court until Mansoul shall realise and acknowledge its sin and seek my face again."

This is the way in which the men of Mansoul first began to turn away from Emmanuel. They did not visit him in his palace as before. They did not notice that he no longer came to visit them. Though he still made his love-feasts for them and called them to come, they were full of excuses and did not care to attend. They did not wait, as before, for his counsel, but began to be headstrong and self-confident, thinking that Mansoul was now so strong that nothing could ever change its conditions and its foes could never attack it again.

Emmanuel did not withdraw all in a moment, but first sent the Lord Secretary to warn his people that they were following dangerous ways and to forbid them to do those things. Twice he came to them, but each time they were at dinner in Mr False-Security's house and would not even listen to the Lord Secretary who, being grieved, returned to Heart Castle, where he dwelt with Emmanuel. The prince was also grieved, and began to withdraw and this is the way in which he did it. He kept himself very much to himself, although he was still in the town. His speech, if in their company, was not now so friendly or pleasant as it had been before. He no longer sent them dainty things from his table, which, until now, had been one of the marks of his kindness and affection. If they came to visit him, as they occasionally did, they might knock once or twice but he did not seem to notice, whereas, before, he used to run to meet them.

Emmanuel thought, by these means, to make his people realise what they were doing and return to him. But none of these things made Mansoul notice, or think upon their present condition or upon their prince's past goodness to them. Therefore he withdrew, first from his palace, then to the gate of the town and finally right away from Mansoul altogether, until they should acknowledge their wrongdoing and earnestly seek his face again. Mr God's-Peace also laid down his commission and retired from the town when Emmanuel withdrew. Alas! the people of Mansoul were by now so hardened in the ways of Mr False-Security, that they did not even notice the withdrawing of their prince, nor realise that they no longer enjoyed his presence.

One day, this crafty Diabolonian made a feast for the chief men of the town and, amongst those whom he invited, was a man called Mr Godly-Fear; no-one thought much of him in these days, although he had once been a great favourite. While all the other guests were feasting and drinking and thoroughly enjoying themselves, it was noticeable that Mr Godly-Fear sat like a stranger and would not join in the merry-making at all. At length, Mr False-Security addressed him:

Mr False-Security: "Mr Godly-Fear, are you not well? I think you must be ill in body or mind, or both? Why do you not join in with all the others? I have a tonic in my cupboard, made up by Mr Forget-Good; let me give you a small taste of that and perhaps you will feel better."

Mr Godly-Fear: "Thank you, sir, but I am not ill and I do not wish to take such a tonic. I cannot join in with your merry-making for I am very perturbed." (Turning to the elders and chiefs of Mansoul), "Gentlemen, I marvel to see you so merry and jolly when Mansoul is in such a serious condition!"

Mr False-Security: "O you poor fellow! You are tired, I

can see that and so you are cast down and depressed. Take a little rest, sir; then you will feel better and you will be able to join us in our feasting."

Mr Godly-Fear: (Ignoring Mr False-Security and speaking still to the men of Mansoul). "I have heard you boasting with this man, of the strength and security of our town. It is true that Mansoul was very strong but you, by your behaviour, have weakened your town more than you realise. I tell you plainly, you have become puffed up with pride through listening to your new friend. You have offended Emmanuel with your coldness of heart and your self-conceit, and now *he is gone*. If you question my words, tell me this. Where is the Prince Emmanuel? When did you last hear him? When did any of you last see him? You now sit feasting with this Diabolonian monster, but he is not your prince. Enemies from outside could never have harmed you like this but, by your own inward sin, you have brought this terrible happening upon your own heads!"

Mr False-Security: "O rubbish, rubbish! You always were a fearful, timid man. Why do you come and spoil our feast with your gloom and your dismal forebodings? Shame on you!"

Mr Godly-Fear: "I do well to be sad, for the glory has departed from Mansoul. Emmanuel *is gone*! And you, sir, are the man who has driven him away. He is gone, without even telling his nobles that he was going and if *that* is not a mark of his anger, then I know nothing of the ways of godliness. When you men of Mansoul turned away from him, he withdrew from you gradually. You did not even notice, but I saw him go. And now, you boast and talk of your strength, but it is gone I tell you! Without him you can do nothing and since he is departed, you may well turn your feast into a time of weeping and sighing."

Upon hearing this, Mr Conscience, the under-preacher, was very startled and, rising to his feet, he said, "Indeed, my brothers, I am afraid that what Mr Godly-Fear says is true! I, for my part, have not seen my prince for a long time; indeed, I cannot even remember the day. I begin to see that Mansoul is in a very serious condition indeed."

Mr Godly-Fear again asserted, "I assure you, you will not find Emmanuel in Mansoul, search where you will. He is departed from us and it is because the elders principally, but the others also, have rewarded his grace and mercy with base ingratitude and coldness of heart."

Poor Mr Conscience was so stricken by these words, that he looked as though he would fall down dead at the table; and all, except Mr False-Security, looked pale and ill at ease. After a while, as the seriousness of Mr Godly-Fear's words began to weigh upon them, they consulted together, wondering if anything could be done. (The Diabolonian had, by this time, withdrawn from the room, being extremely annoyed at what had taken place.) Remembering, now that it was too late, all that their prince had commanded them to do with any Diabolonians they might find, they took Mr False-Security and burned his house about him, thinking by this to be rid of him for ever.

They then ran, with all speed, to look for their prince Emmanuel but, although they sought him diligently, he was not to be found anywhere in the town. Then, at last, they knew that the words of Mr Godly-Fear were true indeed and that they had driven their prince away by their evil and ungodly ways. At this, they thought they would apply to the Lord Secretary (whom before they had ignored), but he would not agree to speak with them nor even show his face to them. O what a day of gloom and darkness that was! Now, alas, they saw how foolish they had been to listen to the swaggering talk of Mr False-Security and what terrible damage this had done to them. (And what it was yet to cost them they little realised.) One good thing came out of this, however, which was that Mr Godly-Fear was once more held in great respect in the town.

When the next Sunday came, they all went to hear Mr Conscience, the under-preacher, but O! what a convicting sermon he preached. He not only exposed their own sin to Mansoul but trembled himself, crying out as he preached, "O unhappy man that I am, that I should do so wicked a thing; that *I*, whom the prince set up to be a preacher and teacher, should have let myself be led into such evil ways. I should have cried out against it, but I let Mansoul wallow in its sin until Emmanuel was driven quite away!"

At the end of the sermon the people seemed utterly crushed, for there was terrible power in the preaching and they hardly knew how to get back to their homes, or how to face their work during the following week. Very soon after this, there arose a great sickness which spread throughout the town, even the captains and their men being affected. Had Mansoul been attacked by enemies at this time, no-one could have done anything to resist, for everywhere there were pale faces, weak hands and feeble knees. The lovely white garments which Emmanuel had given to his people were now looking dreadful; many were torn and all were in a dirty, neglected, bedraggled condition.

When this sad state of affairs had continued for some time, Mr Conscience called for a day of fasting, that the town might humble itself for its terrible wickedness against the great El Shaddai and his son. He asked Captain Boanerges if he would preach. He agreed and gave a very pointed and searching sermon upon the barren fig-tree, showing the need for repentance and what would happen if repentance were lacking. This sermon, together with their remembrance of the other sermon, made Mansoul tremble again, and quite reduced the town to a state of deep mourning and sorrow. Upon asking Mr Godly-Fear if there was anything that they could do, they were advised to send a humble petition to their offended prince, begging him to turn to them yet again in grace and favour and not to keep his anger for ever.

When the chief men had drawn up the petition, they decided to send it by the mayor, Lord Understanding. But, alas! when he had taken his long journey and arrived at the court of the great king, the gates were all shut and a strict watch set, so that he was obliged to stand outside for a considerable time. At length, a messenger took his petition and carried it to the prince, saying that the Lord Mayor of Mansoul was standing outside the gate, desiring to be admitted into the presence of the king's son. But a dreadful answer came back to him, for the prince would not even see him, but sent this message: "In the time of prosperity Mansoul turned their backs upon me, yet now, in the time of trouble, they call upon me. Let them go, rather, to their friend Mr False-Security and ask him to be their lord and protector!"

This answer cast the Lord Mayor into a state of deepest gloom, as he now realised the awful consequences of making friends with a Diabolonian and he returned, weeping, to Mansoul. When he had told his tale the people all wept with him, dressing themselves in sackcloth and ashes. Once more they called upon Mr Godly-Fear for advice, who said, "There is nothing better that you can do than to send another petition; and do not be too discouraged if you several times meet with silence or rebuke. It is the way of the wise El Shaddai to make men wait and exercise patience;

and those who are in such great need can surely await his time and pleasure."

This advice put a little courage into Mansoul and they sent again and again and yet again, one petition after another, beseeching Emmanuel to return to Mansoul. Throughout the long, cold and tedious winter hardly a day or even an hour went by, when one messenger or another might not be seen hastening out of Mouth Gate, bound for the court of El Shaddai.

Chapter Thirteen

The Plotting of the Enemy

You will remember that after the remodelling of the town by Emmanuel there were still quite a few Diabolonians lurking in various hiding places, men like Lord Murder, Lord Anger and Lord Blasphemy, not forgetting Lord Covetousness. You will also remember that the prince had strictly charged his people to hunt these men out, with others equally vile, and slay them, for they were enemies of the prince and those who, if left alive, would not hesitate to work for the ruin of Mansoul. Because the townsmen had not bothered to do as their prince had commanded, these lurking Diabolonians now began to show their heads, coming out of their hiding places and mingling with the people, and what became of this I will now proceed to tell you.

These Diabolonian lords knew quite well that it was because Mansoul had sinned and offended their prince that he had withdrawn from them. They began, therefore, to plot together for the ruin of the town, meeting in the house of a man called Mr Mischief, whose very name marks him as a fellow Diabolonian. It did not take them long to decide that this would be the ideal time to send a letter to Diabolus, asking his advice on their present situation. This is how their letter read:

"O our great father and mighty Prince Diabolus, dwelling in the caves of gloom and darkness, we, the true Diabolonians remaining in the rebellious town of Mansoul, cannot be content to see how you are disgraced and reproached in this place; and what is more, we long for your presence.

"Now, the reason for our writing is that these townspeople have offended their prince Emmanuel so that he has departed from the town and, although they send to him again and again, he will not return to them. Many are now sick and weakly, not only the common people, but also the leaders and captains. Only those of us who are true Diabolonians are strong and lively and we think, if it agrees with your horrible cunning, that it would be good for you to make a further attack upon Mansoul at the present time. In the event of your doing this we, for our part, will do all in our power to deliver the town into your hands."

This letter was sent by the hand of Mr Cursing. Diabolus and his companions were, of course, filled with a most evil joy at receiving this letter and when the death-bell had tolled for some time (which was their way of rejoicing) Diabolus held a consultation with his companions in wickedness. After they had all had their say, they decided to leave the issue with Diabolus who then drew up the following letter in reply.

"My dear children and disciples, my Lords Anger, Murder, Blasphemy and the rest of you, from your Lord Diabolus, true prince of Mansoul.

"Your letter has given great joy both to me and to all who dwell here in this horrible den. We are truly delighted to hear of the miserable condition of the rebellious town; that they have offended their prince and that so many of them are weak and sickly, while you yourselves are in such a flourishing condition. Glad would we be to get them into our clutches again and we will spare neither effort nor cunning to bring this to pass. We will, therefore, do as you suggest and make a surprise attack. Will you, on your part, do all that you can to spy out the weakness of the town? Try to undermine it from within, by tempting the townsmen either to a vain or loose life, or to doubt and despair, or even to blowing up the town with the gunpowder of pride and conceit. Finally, be ready, yourselves, to make a violent assault within the town whenever you learn of our attack from without. That we may work together to a happy conclusion is the desire of your prince and Mansoul's enemy,

Diabolus."

This letter was taken back to the Diabolonians in Mr Mischief's house, by the same Mr Cursing, where it was received with pleasure and its contents considered with great care. After various suggestions had been made, Mr Deceit gave his advice.

"You recall that in this letter from our Prince Diabolus we were advised of three ways in which we might undermine these people: namely, by leading them into a vain and loose life, by tempting them to doubt and despair, or by inciting them to blow up the town. Now, in my opinion, the second suggestion is the best of all. If we can drive them to despair, they will then question whether their prince really loves them, which will surely fill him with disgust. If this works, they will soon stop sending petitions to him, especially when he does not answer, for they will say, 'We might as well do nothing since it is all to no purpose.' "

To achieve this end, it was recommended that certain of the Diabolonians should disguise themselves as workmen from the country and, coming into the market-place on market day, hire themselves out as servants. Then, once within the houses of Mansoul, they could more easily carry on this work of corrupting Mansoul yet further and further. This plan was carried out and before long another letter was on its way to Diabolus, telling him how well his trusted servants were succeeding and suggesting that he should attack the town on a market day with an army of Doubters.

"For," continued the letter, "it is a well-known fact that when people are busy with their worldly affairs they least expect a surprise attack and they will be the least able to defend themselves. Also, it would be easier for us to gather together, unnoticed, on a market day."

While these diabolical plans were going backwards and forwards, Mansoul was still in a most woeful condition. This was partly because they had so grievously offended their King Shaddai, but even more so because, although they had sent so many petitions to him, still Emmanuel had not favoured them with even one smile. Everything was growing blacker and blacker, and their prince seemed to be further away than ever. There was still much sickness in the town, while every day the enemies now present amongst them were becoming stronger and livelier.

When the second letter arrived at the den of Diabolus, he and his companions considered all the news and each had various suggestions to make. Some felt that it would be well to continue as they had been doing, saying, "There is no better way of destroying a soul than by leading it into vile and filthy ways. If our servants can make Mansoul continue like this, the townsmen will soon forget their precious Emmanuel and will no longer desire his company; and if we can make them live like that, he will not come to them in a hurry. For do we not know well that two or three Diabolonians entertained within the town of Mansoul will do more to keep Emmanuel away than a whole army of soldiers could do from outside the town?"

But the rage and hatred of Diabolus could not be held back while these long-term plans came to fruition. He insisted that another attack must be made immediately and that he would lead it again, this time with an army of twenty or thirty thousand Doubters. That was the message which Mr Cursing finally took back to the plotting Diabolonians in Mr Mischief's house, while the evil prince began to beat up his hateful drum, calling his thousands of Doubters to his aid.

So now we see these poor, miserable inhabitants of Mansoul having offended their prince so that he had gone from them and, by their foolishness, having encouraged the powers of hell to come against them, seeking their utter destruction. True, they now realised something of their sin, but their enemies were *within* them; and call though they did to Emmanuel, he would not come to their aid. Perhaps he never would return to them now; and all the while Mansoul languished and grew weaker and weaker, the Diabolonians grew stronger and yet more virile. The petitions were still sent daily, but the townsmen made no real attempt to reform their ways and, as Diabolus knew even if they did not, while they regarded iniquity in their heart, Emmanuel would not hear them.

Chapter Fourteen

The Miseries of Back-Sliding

In spite of all these dreadful plottings, however, and as the wise El Shaddai would have it, there was one person in Mansoul who had the welfare of the town very much upon his heart. His name was Mr True-Concern and he was always watching and listening in case harm should come to the town he loved. Now it so happened that one night, as he was walking through the town keeping his eyes and ears open and alert, he passed by a house which had a very bad reputation. Hearing a muttering coming from within, as though several people were in conference together, he paused and crept near to listen. He had not been standing there very long before he heard someone saying, with great confidence, that in a short while now Diabolus would again possess the town. When this happened, the Diabolonians would kill every inhabitant of Mansoul with the sword, as well as the king's captains, and drive the soldiers from the town. The speaker added that he knew, for certain, that there were more than twenty thousand Doubters being prepared by Diabolus to come against Mansoul and it would not be many days before they arrived.

When Mr True-Concern had heard all that he needed to know, he hurried to the house of the Lord Mayor to acquaint him with the serious news which he had just learned. He, in turn, sent immediately for Mr Conscience, who determined to alert the town without delay. He rang the lecture bell, which gathered all the people together and then told them what Mr True-Concern had discovered, urging them to great watchfulness. Mr True-Concern was asked to confirm his story to the people, but they were quickly persuaded of its truth, for he was known to be a man of honesty and integrity.

They were even more convinced when Mr Conscience added, "After all, there is every reason for it to be true, since we have provoked our king to anger and driven Emmanuel out of the town by our sin, as well as having been too friendly with the Diabolonians. Mr True-Concern also gathered, from the conversation he heard, that many letters have been going back and forth between the Diabolonians and their evil master in which our utter destruction has been plotted and organised."

Upon hearing this, the men of Mansoul lifted up their voices and wept. When they had composed themselves, however, they redoubled their petitions to Emmanuel, also pleading with the captains to be in readiness to fight, night or day, should Diabolus attack the town, which seemed more than likely. The captains had always loved Mansoul and they still did, even though the town was now so sickly, weak and impoverished. They said that they were willing to do everything within their power and agreed:

To keep all the gates of Mansoul locked and barred, strictly examining all who came in or went out, in the hope of detecting or capturing the plotters.

To make a strict and thorough search in every house from top to bottom, in every part of the town, to find, if possible, any of the Diabolonians involved in the plot.

That any people found harbouring Diabolonians should be publicly shamed in front of the whole town, as a warning to all the other townspeople.

That a day of public fasting and humiliation should be kept, acknowledging the justice of the prince and their own wickedness against him and his father (it would be concluded that all who did *not* observe this fast were Diabolonians and these would be dealt with accordingly).

That they should unceasingly petition Emmanuel, at the same time reporting to him all that Mr True-Concern had told them; that thanks should be given to Mr True-Concern for seeking the welfare of the town and that an account of his timely help should be sent to the king.

All these things the town of Mansoul diligently performed, dealing very firmly with those Diabolonians that were found. In Mr Mind's house they discovered the Diabolonian called Lord Covetousness (only he had changed his name to Mr Prudent-Thrifty, hoping by this to escape detection). In Lord Willbewill's house was found a particularly evil Diabolonian by the name of Lord Loose-Living (but he, too, had changed his name to Mr Harmless-Fun). When these two evil characters had been handed over to Mr True-Man the jailor, Mr Mind and Lord Willbewill, according to the agreement of the captains, were made to confess their fault publicly in the market-place, which they did with evident shame and sorrow. There were still other Diabolonians in the town but, although their footsteps could be seen and they were often tracked to their very dens and holes, it seemed impossible to lay hands upon them to bring them to justice. At least, however, they could not now walk openly in the town, as they had done before, but were forced to lie low in their hiding places.

Very soon after this, without saying anything to anyone, Mr True-Concern went out scouting in the country of the Doubters and found that Diabolus was almost ready to march. He came speeding back to tell the captains and the town what he had discovered: namely, that old Lord Unbelief, who had an undying spite against Mansoul and longed for revenge, had been put at the head of this army, which consisted of more than twenty thousand Doubters.

When his army was ready to march, Diabolus set forth on a straight course for Mansoul, having some fearful captains in his band. There were Captain Rage, Captain Fury, Captain Damnation, Captain Devourer, Captain No-Ease, Captain Torment, Captain Corruption and Captain Past-Hope! By reason of Mr True-Concern's splendid work, the town had, at least, been alerted to its danger. The captains had had time to set a strong watch at the gates, doubling and trebling their guards, and mounting their slings in very good positions. But in spite of all this, poor Mansoul was sorely afraid at the first appearance of the enemy and at the roaring of their hideous drum. Diabolus began by making a furious attack upon Ear Gate, fondly imagining that his men in the town were waiting to assist him. Finding that this help was not forth-coming (thanks to the vigilance of the captains) and that he was stoutly resisted with well-aimed stones from the golden slings, he was forced to retreat from the town and entrench his men out of reach of the bombardment. This gave Mansoul a little courage, which it sorely needed.

Diabolus now commanded that, every night, his drummer should march around the walls of the town, beating the drum. How Mansoul trembled at this hateful sound! Diabolus hoped to wear the people down until, in utter weariness, they would be willing to surrender; for there is no more terrible sound upon earth than this drum, except the voice of El Shaddai when he speaks. In full view of the town, the evil prince also set up his standard, which showed a fearful picture of a great fiery furnace, with Mansoul burning in the middle of it! After beating the drum, the messenger announced that, if the townsmen would surrender, Diabolus would do them much good; but if they resisted, he would still take them by force, both by fire and by sword. There was no answer to this, for the people had all retired to the castle where the captains were. They remembered only too vividly what it had cost them when they had listened to Diabolus before. The next night, a similar summons came, but still they ventured no reply.

At this point, Mansoul again applied to the Lord Secretary who still dwelt in Heart Castle, begging his advice and help, but he told them that they had both offended Emmanuel and grieved himself and, for the present time, they must get themselves out of the mess they were in.

"Your own wickedness shall correct you," was his answer, "and your backslidings shall reprove you; only so will you learn that it is an evil and bitter thing that you have forsaken your lord and king, and that his fear is not in you."

This answer fell upon them like a millstone, for now the town was indeed in a pitiable state. Their foes were ready to swallow them up and their friends would give them no help. The Lord Mayor and the captains felt, nevertheless, that within this answer there lay some hope that when they had suffered for their sins, they would be saved at last and perhaps Emmanuel would yet come to their help. This gave them fresh courage to attack Diabolus and his army with the slings and cause considerable damage. The captains were longing to do some work for their prince, so they resolved to attack and keep on attacking, since Diabolus had now come within range again; for, as there is nothing so terrible to Mansoul as the sound of the hideous drum, to Diabolus there is nothing so terrible as the well-aimed slings of El Shaddai. This caused the enemy to retreat still further from the town, to the encouragement of the townspeople.

Finding that his captains and men were beaten back by the stones from the golden slings, Diabolus changed his tactics, deciding that he would now see what a little flattery could do. He came, therefore, without the fearful drum, with sugary words and a most peaceable expression pretending, as once before, that he had only the welfare of the town at heart. He reminded them of the happiness they had enjoyed while he had been their prince; he then insinuated that all their troubles and times of darkness had stemmed from the day they revolted against him and that they need not expect to know any peace until they came back to him. If they would return to him, however, he would enlarge their charter and make their days pleasant and easy again.

The Lord Mayor made answer to this lying speech by saying, "O Diabolus, prince of darkness and master of deceit! We have already tasted too deeply of your poisonous cup to listen to your lying flatteries and join with you again. Would not our prince then reject us altogether? We would rather die by your hand than fall in again with your deceit and lies!"

This answer put Diabolus into one of his usual rages. He began beating his hateful drum again, calling up his men to make another assault upon the town, while the men of

Mansoul sounded their silver trumpets and made their preparations for defence. The battle raged for several days, during which time some of the chief men in Mansoul were wounded. Lord Reason was wounded in the head, Lord Understanding had a wound in his eye, Mr Mind was injured near the stomach, while Mr Conscience received a shot very near to the heart. I am glad to say that none of these was a mortal wound, although quite a few of the ordinary people in the town were killed. The enemy also had their casualties; Captain Rage and Captain Fury were wounded and Captain Damnation was forced to retreat. The standard of Diabolus was beaten into the mud when his standard-bearer, Captain Do-much-Harm, had his head crushed in with a stone from one of the slings, to the shame and fury of his prince. Many of the Doubters were killed outright, but this still left enough of them alive to make Mansoul shake and totter. However, the outcome of this battle was to put some fresh hope and courage into Mansoul and to cast a cloud of gloom over the enemy camp.

Mansoul took the opportunity to have a day's rest, ringing the bells and sounding the trumpets to encourage the townspeople, while Lord Willbewill went on his rounds again, hunting for Diabolonians. He had been extraordinarily brave and faithful since he had publicly confessed his fault in the market-place. He managed to capture Mr Anything, whom we have met before and also a deceitful man called Mr Loose-Foot who had been going to and from the enemy camp with messages to the Diabolonians in the town. These were both handed over to Mr True-Man, the jailor. The Lord Mayor could not do very much because of his wound, but continued to send encouraging orders to all the men of the town, while Mr Conscience did his utmost to keep all his good teaching alive in the hearts of the people of Mansoul.

Chapter Fifteen

Diabolus Regains Entry

It was about this time that the captains and bravest men in Mansoul decided to make a sortie to the enemy camp; but they would do this at night. In this lay their folly, because darkness is the best time for the enemy to fight, but the very worst time for Mansoul. Their last victory having raised their courage, however, they were determined to make this attempt. Lots were cast to see who should go on this expedition and they fell to Captain Faith, Captain Experience and Captain Good-Hope.

Forth went these three with their men and happened to

fall in quite soon with the main body of their enemies. Now of course, Diabolus and his men were experts in fighting at night-time, however dark it might be (in fact the darker the better for them), so they quickly and easily set about the captains. These fought very bravely, wounding many of the Diabolonians and causing them to retreat; but somehow, as they were pursuing hard behind their enemies, Captain Faith stumbled and fell, hurting himself so severely that he could not rise until Captain Experience came to his aid.[1] His injury was so grievous that he could not help giving a loud cry of pain, which greatly weakened the other two captains when they heard it, for they imagined that their brother captain had been mortally wounded. Diabolus, seeing that the pursuit had ceased for some reason, came back and set about the captains cutting and wounding them to such an extent that, what with their wounds and the loss of blood, it was as much as they and their men could do to get safely back to Mansoul.

Diabolus was rather pleased with this night's work and promised himself that, within a few days, he would win an easy victory over the town. He sent a message with great boldness, demanding that the town surrender to his government forthwith.

But the Lord Mayor answered him bravely, saying, "As long as our Emmanuel is alive, although he does not yet appear for our help, we will never surrender to you."

Lord Willbewill also answered, "O Diabolus, master of the den of iniquity and enemy of all that is noble and good, we are too well acquainted with your rule to submit to you again. Although we did once submit to you, now that we have been turned from darkness to light, we have also been turned from your power to the power of El Shaddai.

[1] When faith falters, it is the remembrance of past experience of blessing that enables it to stand firm again.

And, although by our own fault and your subtlety, we are now in a sorry plight, yield to you we will not! We will die rather but we have hopes that help will even yet be sent to us from the court of our king."

This brave speech, together with that of the Lord Mayor, not only deflated the tyrant somewhat, but put great strength into the wounded captains, especially Captain Faith, who always loves a brave speech for the truth.

I should have mentioned that, while the captains were making their sortie into the fields, the Diabolonians within Mansoul had thought this an ideal time to stir up the town and make an uproar. But they had reckoned without Lord Willbewill who was now always on the look-out for Diabolonians. He fell upon them with his men, cutting and slashing them with a furious zeal; so much so, that, although it cannot be said that any were actually killed outright, many (such as Lord Argument and Lord Murmuring) were thankful to hide away quickly, having had quite enough of Willbewill's heavy hand and the edge of his penetrating sword. This brave act did at least avenge the wrong done by Diabolus to the three captains and also let the enemy know that Mansoul was not to be won as easily as they had imagined.

Nevertheless, Diabolus urged his men to attack yet again and somehow, that night, they managed to break through at Feel Gate, which was always a little weak and the most easily made to yield. Captain No-Ease and Captain Torment were immediately put in charge here. Emmanuel's captains resisted as well as they could and with great courage but, with their three best men wounded and their own hands absolutely full of Doubters, the onslaught was more than they could cope with. When they saw that Diabolus was actually in the town, the captains and the prince's men retired speedily to the castle, partly for their own safety, but chiefly to keep it from Diabolus and yet preserve it for Emmanuel.

The evil followers of Diabolus, meeting with little or no resistance, swarmed through the town after their prince, turning the people out of their houses, even out of their beds, and abusing them very badly. Mr Conscience's house was as full of Doubters as it could possibly be. So was the home of Lord Willbewill and the Lord Mayor's palace. The town seemed now to be a veritable den of devils and a place of thick darkness, for nothing could be heard but the battle-cry "*Hell-Fire*", to the accompaniment of the hideous drum. Poor Mansoul! Now it was tasting the bitter fruits of its sin; now it was realising what hidden poison there had been in the flattering words of Mr False-Security.

The Diabolonians worked havoc wherever they went, for they did not know the meaning of the words mercy or pity. Many of the townsmen were wounded, Mr Conscience among them. He lay in continual pain night and day and, except that El Shaddai over-rules all things, no doubt he would have been killed outright. Lord Understanding almost had his eyes put out and, had Lord Willbewill not escaped into the castle, he would have been chopped up in pieces, for the Diabolonians hated him more than any other. Diabolonians swarmed in every corner, so that in all parts of the town could be heard hideous noises, vain songs, lying stories and blasphemous language against El Shaddai and his son. All the lurking Diabolonians now came out boldly, and, in company with the Doubters, swaggered through the town as if they owned it.

Yet, for all this, Diabolus was not very happy, for he could not regain possession of Heart Castle; nor were he and his men treated as the captains and forces of Emmanuel had been, for the townspeople did everything they could to show their dislike of their enemies. They gave them nothing willingly, but hid everything they possibly could out of the reach of their grasping hands. They plainly showed that they would rather have their room than their company but, since for the present they were captives, they would bear it with as bad a grace as they dared. The captains in the castle continued to send some well-aimed missiles upon their enemies from the golden slings and, although Diabolus made repeated and vicious attempts upon the castle, he was as often repulsed. Mr Godly-Fear had been made keeper of the castle gate and he was so full of courage and vigour that, as long as he was alive, there was no hope of ever getting past him. (This good man would have made an excellent governor of the whole town!)

Well, this wretched, divided condition lasted for about two and a half years and the glory of Mansoul was laid low in the dust. One day, however, the elders of the town were gathered together, bemoaning their pitiable condition, when someone suggested that they ought to send yet another petition to their prince. As they were thinking how to word it, Mr Godly-Fear stopped them. He said that he now remembered that his lord the prince never would receive a petition that was not signed by the Lord Secretary and he thought that it was probably for this reason that all their previous petitions had been unsuccessful. His advice was that they should go to the Lord Secretary and ask him to draw up a new petition for them and put his signature to it, for the prince never failed to recognise his handwriting.

The elders thanked Mr Godly-Fear very heartily for his good advice and went with all haste to the castle to see the Lord Secretary. They asked him if he would be pleased to draw up a petition for them, signing it himself, so that they could send it to Emmanuel, since Mansoul was now in such a deplorable condition.

"And what kind of petition do you expect me to draw up

for you?" asked the Lord Secretary.

"O my lord, you know that best yourself," answered the elders, "for you are aware of the backslidden state of this town. You know who has come to make war against us and of the cruel way in which so many of the townspeople have been treated. Will you not, therefore, draw it up for us?"

"Very well," said the Lord Secretary, "I will do that for you and I will set my seal to it."

"When may we call for it, my lord?" they asked.

"O, you must be present at the writing of it," was the answer, "and you must put your desires into it. The handwriting and the pen shall be mine, but the paper and the ink must be yours, else how can it be called your petition? I have no need to petition for myself for I have not offended. I will not send a petition to the prince and, by him, to his father, unless the people involved are in the matter heart and soul."

The elders quite saw the point of this, so the petition was drawn up as the Lord Secretary had suggested. But who should take it for them? It was he, again, who suggested that it should be sent by the hand of Captain Faith, who, when asked if he would be willing to do this, replied that he would gladly take it and with as much speed as possible, in view of his lameness – (resulting, of course, from his old wounds, which still troubled him).

This is how the new petition read:

> "O our lord and sovereign Emmanuel, the long-suffering prince, to you belong mercy and forgiveness though we have rebelled against you.
>
> We, who are no longer fit to be called your Mansoul, do yet beseech you to come and do away with our sins and wickedness. O lord, do it for your own name's sake, for to whom can we turn if not to you? Our captains are weak and sick and our enemies are strong and lively. Our wis-

dom is gone and our power is gone, because you have departed from us. We have nothing to call our own but our sin, and we are filled with shame and confusion of face. O lord, take pity upon your miserable, wretched Mansoul and come and save us out of the hand of our enemies. Amen."

This petition was delivered to Captain Faith, who hurried out of Mouth Gate, carrying it with as much speed as possible to Emmanuel.

Now somehow, I do not know how, news of the sending of this petition came eventually to the ears of Diabolus, who ground his teeth in anger, saying to himself "O rebellious Mansoul, I will make you stop sending these petitions."

He ordered his drum to be beaten unceasingly, for he knew how Mansoul loathed the sound of it, at the same time stirring up his followers to do yet more and more wicked and cruel things to all the remaining people in the town. Before his spiteful orders could be carried out, however, he marched audaciously up to the castle gate demanding, upon pain of death, that it should be opened to him immediately. Mr Godly-Fear, of course, answered that nothing would ever induce him to open the gate and that he was confident that after Mansoul had suffered a while, it would be made perfect, strengthened and settled.

"Well then," said Diabolus, "deliver into my hands the men who have petitioned against me, especially that evil Captain Faith who has dared to take your petition to the king. Give him up to me and I will promise to depart from your town."

Up jumped one of the Diabolonians, Mr Fooling by name, saying, "My lord offers you a fair deal. Is it not better to give up Captain Faith for the sake of the town, than that all of you should perish?"

"No, indeed," said the valiant Mr Godly-Fear. "How long do you suppose Mansoul will last when it has once given up its faith to Diabolus? We may as well lose the town if we are to lose our Captain Faith."

To this the Lord Mayor added, "Know this for certain, O tyrant, that we are determined to resist you as long as there is a captain, a man, a sling, or even a stone left in the town."

"O you fools," screamed Diabolus, almost dancing with rage, "do you still think that your Emmanuel will come to your aid? You have been too wicked for him to listen to your prayers. Do you not realise that not only I, but he is against you? It is he who has sent me to subdue you. What are you yet hoping for? How do you think you can escape?"

Unhesitatingly, the Lord Mayor answered him, "We have sinned indeed (and how we have suffered for it), but our Emmanuel has said, and that with all faithfulness, 'him that cometh unto me I will in no wise cast out'. He has also told us, O enemy of Mansoul, that all manner of sin and blasphemy shall be forgiven to the sons of men. We do not despair, therefore, but we will still look for, hope for and wait for deliverance."

While this commotion was taking place at the castle gate, news came that Captain Faith had returned from the court of the king *with a sealed package*! The Lord Mayor left Diabolus to go on shouting at the castle wall, if he had a mind to, while he hurried away to find Captain Faith. There were tears in his eyes, so great were his longing and hoping, as he asked the good Captain Faith if there was a message from Emmanuel at last.

"Be of good cheer, my lord," said the Captain, "all will be well in time."

He then produced the package, which he put on one side until all the elders could be assembled; but even this seemed a hopeful sign to the waiting men and captains. When at last they were all gathered, the Captain opened the package, drawing out several notes.

The first was addressed to the Lord Mayor, Lord Understanding, saying that Emmanuel was pleased that he had been so trustworthy in his office and so deeply concerned about the welfare of Mansoul. He was pleased with his bold and forthright speaking against Diabolus on behalf of his prince and indicated that he would shortly receive his reward.

The second was for Lord Willbewill, telling him that Emmanuel knew well how courageous he also had been for the honour of his prince, now absent, even when his name was held in contempt by Diabolus. He was pleased with the brave way in which he had personally dealt with so many of the Diabolonians and he, too, might expect a reward before long.

The third note was sent to Mr Conscience, the underpreacher, assuring him that Emmanuel was well aware how faithfully he had fulfilled his office, exhorting, rebuking and forewarning Mansoul according to the laws of the town; also, how he had called the town to fasting, sackcloth and ashes. A reward would also be coming for him.

The fourth note came for Mr Godly-Fear, in which his prince noted that he was the first man in Mansoul to detect Mr False-Security's corrupting effect upon the town, exposing him in his own house. The prince still remembered his tears and mourning over the state of Mansoul. He knew that Mr Godly-Fear had most bravely defended Heart Castle against the tyrant, and that it was he who had shown the townsmen how to address their petition to the prince for its acceptance. His reward, too, would soon be forthcoming.

Finally, there was a note addressed to the whole town of Mansoul itself. Their lord prince told them that he was not unaware of their continued petitioning and that they should see the fruit of this before long. He knew that now, at last, their heart and mind were firmly fixed in his ways, although Diabolus had made such inroads upon them; that now, neither flatteries on the one hand, nor threats and hardships on the other, could make them yield to his evil designs. The note ended with a reminder that the town was to be left in the hands of the Lord Secretary and, under him, Captain Faith, and if Mansoul would carefully yield to their governing and direction, it would not be long before they were rewarded also.

O! what comfort and hope filled the hearts of all who listened to the reading of these messages! At last it seemed that their petitions had been heard and who could tell what Emmanuel might now do for them?

After Captain Faith had delivered his messages, he went straight to the Lord Secretary's dwelling, there to have sweet fellowship with him; for you must know that Captain Faith was always a great favourite with the Lord Secretary, who loved him dearly, and these two together knew more of what was likely to happen to Mansoul than any others in the town. Indeed, Captain Faith seemed able to obtain an interview with the Lord Secretary even when the whole of the town was under his displeasure.

It was only a short while after this that the Lord Secretary made Captain Faith lieutenant over all the prince's forces, so that none could come or go without his consent. He was now to be supreme commander in the war that still raged between Diabolus and Mansoul. When the townspeople saw what easy access Captain Faith had, both to the Lord Secretary and to the court of the king, and what a favourite he evidently was, they heartily wished that they had made more use of him before this in their time of distress. They then sent Mr Conscience to the Secretary, saying that the town greatly desired that Captain Faith should govern them in all matters from this time onward, to which he replied that this should be so and nothing would please him more.

But all these undertakings which I have just related to you were performed with the utmost secrecy, for the enemy was still terribly strong in the town.

Chapter Sixteen

The Return of the Longed-for Prince

To return to Diabolus. Finding himself so boldly confronted both by the Lord Mayor and Mr Godly-Fear, he fell into one of his customary rages which resulted in yet another evil council. The main issue which he brought before his followers was; how to regain possession of Heart Castle, because they could hardly consider themselves masters of the town while the castle was still in the hands of their enemies.

It was Apollyon who first suggested withdrawing from the town. He said that, quite obviously, they were never going to succeed while the castle was occupied by so many brave captains and while the bold Mr Godly-Fear was in charge of the gate.

"When we have withdrawn," said this crafty one, "they will be glad of a respite and will begin to relax; then they may begin to sin, which will be the biggest damage of all. Our withdrawing might also draw the captains out after us which would be to our advantage, for we can fight them better in the open field than cramped here in the town. We may even be able to ambush them and then rush in again to take possession of the castle."

Beelzebub then stood up and replied, "So far, so good, but we shall never be able to draw all the captains away from the castle and the ruse will quite fail unless we can get all of them to follow us."

It certainly seemed as though the first part of Apollyon's advice was the most likely to succeed—that when the enemy had withdrawn, the townsmen would begin to relax and perhaps soon begin to sin again, so bringing about their own destruction. All the members of the council agreed that the surest way to get into the castle was to make the people sin afresh against Emmanuel, for as long as they could call to him they could never be completely defeated.

Lucifer then made his suggestion. "We are all agreed to withdraw from the town and leave the people to relax. Let us take care not to frighten them any more, either with threats, or with the drum which they hate, nor to send any more summonses to them, for it seems that the more they are frightened, the harder they fight. Now the next step, I suggest, is this: since Mansoul is a market town and one that delights in trading, let us send in some Diabolonians to trade with them each market day. We could send cunning men like Mr Love-this-present-World and Mr Easy-Gain; they are crafty rogues and our true friends and can easily be dressed as though they had come from a far country. When the men of Mansoul become more and more taken up with business, when they become full and rich, then we shall get them. You remember how well this succeeded with Laodicea and how many we hold at present in this snare. When they are rich and comfortable and begin to forget their misery, they will become neglectful and careless and will not watch the town gates, or the castle gate, so carefully. Indeed, if we can really fill the town with merchandise, they may even have to store it in the castle, so that it might become, in time, more like a warehouse than a stronghold! Then, when we attack, it will be difficult for the captains to retreat there and much more difficult to defend. Is there not a proverb that says, 'the deceitfulness of riches chokes the word' and 'when the heart is full of drunkenness and the cares of this life, mischief comes upon them unawares'?"

This idea of choking Mansoul with the good things of this life was regarded as a masterpiece of hellish cunning and the meeting broke up, confident of ultimate success.

But, see how things are over-ruled and made to work together for good by the wise El Shaddai! At this very time a letter came to Captain Faith from Emmanuel himself saying that, on the third day from now, he would meet Captain Faith on the field in the plains around Mansoul.

"Meet me on the field?" puzzled the Captain. "Now what does my lord mean by that message?"

So he took his letter straightaway to the Lord Secretary, seeking his advice, for he knew all things that concerned the great king and his son. After a pause, having read the letter through, the Lord Secretary said slowly, "I happen to know that the Diabolonians have just held a council together, contriving the further ruin of Mansoul. The result of this is that they will withdraw from the town, setting plans afoot to make Mansoul destroy itself. They intend to lie in wait in the plains until their plans mature. Now, if you and your captains are ready early on the third day to attack the Diabolonians, your prince will then also be in the field of battle with a mighty force, thus trapping the enemy between the two armies."

Captain Faith was delighted with this information and went to tell the other captains that the message which had seemed so puzzling to him had been clearly explained by the Lord Secretary. The captains also were glad when they heard the strategy put forward and ordered the silver trumpets of the king to be sounded forth from the battlements of the castle.

Diabolus and his fellows were greatly perplexed at this music, wondering what it might mean. "They are sounding neither 'Boot-and-saddle' nor 'Horse-and-away' nor yet 'A charge'," mused the tyrant. "There is a triumphant note in that music which I do not like to hear."

"I shouldn't be surprised," said one of his companions gloomily, "if it means that they have heard that their precious Emmanuel is coming for their relief at last at the head of a great army."

This made all the Diabolonians look glum, but they decided to keep to their original plan and quit the town, because, even if Emmanuel should be coming, they felt they could fight him better on the open plain than risk being trapped in the town. So, on the second day, they withdrew their forces from Mansoul, but set themselves in a formidable manner before Eye Gate, taking care to be well out of reach of the hated golden slings.

Eager preparations were being made by all the king's captains within Mansoul, for Captain Faith's words, "You shall see your prince in the field tomorrow", were like oil added to a fire; it seemed so long since they had seen him and they could hardly wait to get started. When all was ready and the third day had come, before it was properly light, Captain Faith went to the head of his waiting army and passed the battle-cry to his fellow captains. They in turn passed it to their under-officers; it was "*The sword of Prince Emmanuel and the shield of Captain Faith*".[1] The captains then rode out of the town and, falling to, attacked the Diabolonian force from behind, in front and all round.

Now they had left Captain Experience at home because he was still suffering from wounds received in his last fight. But when he saw the captains depart, he called for his crutches, crying, "Shall I lie here while my brother captains are fighting for the life of Mansoul and when Emmanuel, my prince, will show himself in the field to his servants?"

Strangely enough, the sight of Captain Experience on his crutches, far from causing the enemy to mock, roused fear in their hearts, for they thought, "Whatever spirit of courage has possessed Mansoul now, that they will fight us even on crutches?"

Well, the fighting began and, at first, Diabolus hoped that nothing more would come than blows and strokes from their two-edged swords.[2] He was hard beset defending himself, for both Captain Faith and Lord Willbewill attacked him and the Doubters who were around him, and Willbewill's blows were like those of an angry giant. Then the Lord Secretary commanded that the slings from the castle should be set in operation and these greatly added to the confusion all round. Soon, however, the men who were fleeing from the captains began to rally again and fell upon the rear of the pursuing army. The captains' men were beginning to grow faint and weary, until they suddenly remembered that they would soon see the face of their prince; this immediately gave them fresh courage, so that they were able to fight back very fiercely. When there was a

[1] Or as we would say, "*The Word of God and Faith*".
[2] The Word of God.

pause the captains shouted the battle-cry again, "*The sword of Prince Emmanuel and the shield of Captain Faith*", and at this, the Diabolonians fell back, thinking that reinforcements had arrived – but no Emmanuel as yet appeared. The battle seemed to come to something of a halt here, as both sides retreated a space to re-form themselves, so Captain Faith took this opportunity of addressing his men.

"Gentlemen soldiers and my brothers in combat, it rejoices me to see such a valiant army of men fighting today for their love of Mansoul. You have shown yourselves true men of courage against Diabolus so that, for all his boasting, he has gained no advantage over us yet. Stir yourselves, my men, and make this second attack upon the enemy; for then Emmanuel will surely come and you will see your prince in person."

No sooner had the noble captain ended this encouraging speech than a messenger, Mr Speedy, galloped in, post-haste, to say that Emmanuel was at hand! Hearing this, the captains and men were like those raised from the dead and they set upon the enemy once more, shouting their battle-cry aloud as they went.

Many Doubters were killed in this attack, while the battle raged from side to side. When he had been in the heat of the fighting for an hour or so, Captain Faith lifted his eyes and behold! there was Emmanuel, the golden prince, riding in, his colours flying above his head. With such speed did they come towards the part of the battle where the captains were fighting so bravely that the feet of his men seemed hardly to touch the ground. Emmanuel soon joined up with Captain Faith and together they mercilessly beat down the enemy all around them. When the captains and their men saw that their longed-for prince had come and that Captain Faith and he were conquering so gloriously, they gave a mighty shout of triumph, "*The sword of Prince Emmanuel and the shield of Captain Faith*", which made the earth shake and the hearts of the enemy grow cold with fear.

Seeing that the battle was now going seriously against them, what did Diabolus and his evil lordly companions do, but escape hastily towards their den, forsaking their army of Doubters and leaving them to fall by the hand of the prince and his royal army? At the finish, there was not so much as one Doubter left alive, they lay all over the battle-field, slain.

As soon as the battle was ended, at the earliest possible moment, the captains and elders of Mansoul gathered around Emmanuel to greet him and to welcome him with a thousand welcomes, so glad were they to see their beloved prince once more in the vicinity of his Mansoul.

He, in turn, smiled upon them, saying, "My peace be upon you all".

The gates of the town were flung wide open for his reception and he went up before them all, riding in his silver and purple chariot, with his golden armour gleaming in the sun. All the while the silver trumpets were sounding forth and the brilliant colours of the men and of the prince streamed gaily in the wind. Many of the elders had, by this time, lined themselves beside Eye Gate and, as he approached, they began to sing,

"Lift up your heads, O ye gates,
And be ye lift up ye everlasting doors,
And the king of glory shall come in."

Then some sang,

"Who is this king of glory?"

and others answered,

"The lord, strong and mighty,
The lord, mighty in battle,
He is the king of glory."

Singers and players on musical instruments went before

the prince and all his captains accompanied him. When he came into the town, he found the streets were decked with flowers and branches and as he passed by all the people cried aloud with joy, "Blessed be our prince who comes in the name of his father, the great El Shaddai".

At the castle gate, the chief men were waiting to receive their prince: the Lord Mayor, Lord Willbewill, Mr Conscience, Mr Knowledge, Mr Mind and others. They bowed down before him, kissing the dust at his feet and thanking him that he had not held their sins against them but, taking pity on their misery, had returned to build up his Mansoul with blessings forever. So he entered once again into his royal palace, Heart Castle, which had been kept for him, during his absence, by the Lord Secretary and Captain Faith. All the people of the town followed him to the castle and, bowing down before him, wept and lamented over their sin which had driven him out of the town. They begged that he would forgive them and once again affirm his love for his Mansoul.

To this the great prince replied, "Do not weep my people, but go to your houses and feast and be glad, for 'the joy of the lord is your strength'. I have returned to Mansoul full of mercies and I intend that my name shall be exalted and magnified in this place."

He then took many of them in his arms, giving them the royal kisses of his pardon and love. He also gave to the elders chains of gold and signets, and sent earrings and jewels to their wives and children.

"Go and wash your garments in the fountain opened for all uncleanness," he commanded them, "and then come to me again within my castle."

When they had carefully washed their garments, making them white once more, they came and stood again before their prince. Now, after such a long time of darkness and misery, there was music and dancing throughout the whole of Mansoul, for the prince had again granted them his gracious presence, which was the light and joy of their eyes. The bells rang out, the sun shone down upon the happy town and, once more, it was a place of sweetness and delight.

Lord Willbewill was now a greater terror than ever before to the Diabolonians who were still hiding within the town, rooting them out and putting them to death with unparalleled zeal. When the town was more in order, the prince sent trusted men to bury the Doubters who lay in the fields outside the walls of the town. They were instructed to bury every bone, or skull, so that not even the smallest trace of a Diabolonian Doubter might ever be found near Mansoul again, but that their name should be blotted out from under heaven.

Finally, Mr God's-Peace came back to the town, gladly taking up his old commission amongst them again.

Chapter Seventeen

Diabolus Routed At Last

You will hardly credit it when I tell you that, after all this, Diabolus would still not admit himself defeated, but began to plot and plan yet again with Lord Unbelief and his other companions in wickedness, to see how they could be revenged upon Mansoul and Emmanuel. The upshot of this was that he raised another army, composed this time of ten thousand Doubters and fifteen thousand Bloodthirsty Men (and in the latter he put great confidence).

The Doubters, as I should perhaps have told you before, were so called because they came from the land of Doubting (which lies between the land of Darkness and the Valley of the Shadow of Death) and because it is their inborn nature to put a question upon every truth or promise uttered by either Emmanuel or El Shaddai. The Bloodthirsty Men (coming from the land of Loathe-Good) were also just as their name implies and they are always in league with the Doubters. Their captains have such names as Captain Cain, Captain Ishmael, Captain Esau, Captain Saul, Captain Absalom and Captain Judas. These men were cruel villains indeed, with no feelings of compunction or pity; men who would not hesitate to kill father, mother or friend, especially if this would help to line their pockets or advance their worldly position. Captain Cain was over the murdering and angry bands; Captain Ishmael was over the mocking and scorning bands; Captain Esau over the revengeful men, who also grudged others a blessing; Captain Saul over the groundlessly-jealous and madly-furious bands; Captain Absalom over those who would kill father or friend for personal preferment and Captain Judas over the men who could speak as friends and then betray to death.

So, once again, Diabolus led his army against Mansoul. This time he put most of his faith in the Bloodthirsty Men, for the Doubters had already suffered a bad defeat in the previous war. He thought that these fresh warriors might be useful in backing up the main band if occasion demanded. The Bloodthirsty Men were seldom known to return from a battle empty-handed, but were like mastiffs for fastening on to the enemy. Diabolus found, to his dismay, that he was unable to surprise the town as he had hoped, because the faithful Mr True-Concern had been out scouting again, so giving Mansoul plenty of warning of the army's approach. By the time the enemy had arrived, the gates were shut and guarded, and the townsmen alerted for defence. There was nothing for Diabolus to do but set the Doubters opposite Feel Gate, and the Bloodthirsty Men against Eye Gate and Ear Gate.

Lord Unbelief was once more in supreme charge of the attacking army and, in the name of his prince, he sent a red-hot summons to the town, threatening that if it did not surrender immediately, it could expect to be burnt to the ground. The men of Mansoul, however, had learned their lesson at last, knowing better than to act without advice, so that, after reading the summons through, they took it at once to their prince, writing at the bottom, "Lord prince, save Mansoul from these Bloodthirsty Men who cry for our destruction".

The prince read the summons, noting the pathetic appeal at its foot. He then sent Captain Faith and Captain Patience to the part of Mansoul that was now besieged by the Bloodthirsty Men, while Captain Good-Hope, Captain Love and Lord Willbewill he detailed to take charge of the other side of the town to watch over the Doubters. He then set up his standard upon the battlements of the castle, commanding Captain Experience to draw up his men and exercise them daily in the market-place in the sight of all the people, for their encouragement.

This latest siege lasted for some long time, many fierce attacks being made by the Bloodthirsty Men, while some of the townsmen and soldiers had quite close skirmishes with them. The most notable one for this was Captain Self-Denial who had been put in command of Ear Gate and Eye Gate at this time. He was only a young man, like Captain Experience, but exceedingly brave. On his second return, Emmanuel had made him captain over a thousand men, for the general good of Mansoul. Being, as I have remarked, a man of great courage, willing always to suffer for the good of Mansoul, Self-Denial would often sally forth upon the Bloodthirsty Men, entering into several exciting engagements with them. They sustained many losses at his hand, but he was not unhurt himself; he bore some deep scars on his body as a result of wounds received in these attacks.

When some time had elapsed, sufficient for Emmanuel thoroughly to try and test the faith, hope and love of Mansoul, on a certain day he called his captains to him and, dividing them into two companies, commanded them to go out early the next morning and fall upon the Doubters and the Bloodthirsty Men. The former they were to slay without mercy, the latter to take alive.

At the time appointed, out from the city went our brave captains, strengthened by the knowledge that, since their prince had sent them, they could not fail while they were acting under his wise command. The Doubters, seeing these formidable men coming against them and remembering how their fellow Doubters had fared the last time they had joined in battle, decided that they would not stay to meet them again. They promptly beat a retreat and fled from the prince's men, who pursued them hotly, killing them in their hundreds, although they could not catch them all. (Those that escaped wandered about for some time afterwards, in bands of varying sizes and would occasionally show themselves to Mansoul; but if either Captain Faith, Captain Experience or Captain Good-Hope so much as showed their faces, the Doubters fled like startled rabbits!)

The Bloodthirsty Men, on the other hand, seeing the captains coming against them, but that Emmanuel himself was not in the field of battle, concluded that this meant that Emmanuel was not in Mansoul after all! This made them rather over-confident and they despised the prince's men, until they found themselves surrounded. They would have run away themselves then, for, although they are cruel and implacable men when they are on the winning side, yet they are cowards at heart and quite ready to run if they find themselves equalled. The captains soon rounded them up and took them back to the prince to be examined by him.

Some of these Bloodthirsty Men had fought out of ignorance, having very little idea of the worth or greatness of the prince, and when they stood before him and saw his majesty they trembled with fear, crying out for mercy. These the prince touched with his golden sceptre, showing them his mercy. Others, however, neither wept nor repented, but stood biting their lips and grinding their teeth in suppressed fury; these the prince bound over to appear at the Great Assize[1] when they would have to answer to King Shaddai for all they had done.

That night, four of the Doubters who escaped managed to creep back into the town unnoticed, seeking refuge in the house of a man called Mr Evil-Questioning (a perpetual enemy of Mansoul), who willingly gave them shelter, pitying their misfortunes. He said that he was most pleased to welcome them as his guests and asked them how it was that they had suffered such a grave defeat in the battle and who their chief captain had been. He was amazed when they told him how Lord Unbelief had fled, but they said this was not really surprising and he could hardly be blamed, for, had he been caught, the men of Mansoul would have hanged him without hesitation.

"Well, that is a great pity," said the evil man. "How I wish that there were ten thousand of you Doubters here in Mansoul and that I might be your leader. What havoc we could cause together."

"So do we wish it," agreed his guests, "but what is the use of wishing?"

"We had better lower our voices," warned Evil-Questioning, "and you must take care that you do not air these sentiments outside this house or you will quickly be caught and dealt with. The prince, the Lord Secretary and all the captains and men are in the town. As for that cruel man

[1] The Judgement Day.

Willbewill, his favourite hobby is catching Diabolonians and putting them to death. He can smell them out like a hunting dog, so be very wary."

Now, unknown to them, all this time one of Willbewill's faithful and most courageous officers, Mr Diligence, had been listening to this conversation under the eaves of the house and when he had heard sufficient, off he went to his master to recount all that he had just overheard. Without delay, Lord Willbewill went along with Mr Diligence, who led him to Mr Evil-Questioning's house.

"Now listen, my lord," said Mr Diligence, "and tell me whether you recognise the voice of Mr Evil-Questioning."

"Yes," said Lord Willbewill after a few moments, "there is no doubt that it is he. To my shame I have to confess that I know his voice well, for he and I were great friends during the reign of the tyrant Diabolus. He is a cunning and crafty man; I only hope we can arrest him before he gives us the slip."

They both listened a little while longer and then, at a signal from Lord Willbewill, Mr Diligence burst open the door and between them they managed to capture the five men who were then led away and put in the charge of Mr True-Man, the jailor.

The Lord Mayor was delighted when he learned that this man, Evil-Questioning, had been seized, for he had long been a source of trouble both in the town and, personally, to the Lord Mayor. Although many had sought for him, no one had ever yet been able to lay hands upon him, or actually to be certain of his dwelling-place. Lord Willbewill had the authority to kill these plotting Diabolonians at once, but he thought that it would be more for the honour of the prince, the comfort of the town and the discouraging of any other Diabolonians, if there were a public trial and execution.

Accordingly, the men were brought before the court in

Mansoul, with the same jury that had tried the other Diabolonians, and Mr Evil-Questioning certainly proved to be a slippery customer, as Lord Willbewill had implied. This was the charge against him: "That he was a Diabolonian by nature, a sworn enemy of Prince Emmanuel and one who had studied the ruin of Mansoul; that he had said openly how he wished there were ten thousand Doubters within the town of Mansoul with himself at their head, and that he had deliberately entertained those who were avowed enemies of the town."

When asked whether he was guilty or not guilty, he replied, "My lord, I do not understand this charge, for I am not the man concerned. My name is not Evil-Questioning but Honest-Enquiry."

This, however, was soon disproved by reliable witnesses, one of whom was Lord Willbewill himself. He acknowledged, with genuine sorrow, that he had once been the intimate friend of this man and that there was no question but that he really *was* Mr Evil-Questioning, a Diabolonian by birth and nature, an enemy of the prince and a hater of Mansoul. When the prisoner was charged with harbouring enemies of the town, he said that he was only being kind to strangers and was it now a crime in Mansoul to help those in need? Why should he be blamed for an act of kindness?

The Lord Mayor answered all his objections, showing that, while it was indeed a virtue to entertain strangers, it was still treason to entertain the king's enemies. He also reminded him that, by reason alone of his being a Diabolonian, he was due to die by the law of the prince, quite apart from the fact that he had received and nourished other Diabolonians.

"O I see," said Evil-Questioning with the air of a martyr, "I am to be made to suffer because of my kindness and charity to those in need!"

The other Diabolonians having been fairly tried and found guilty of crimes against Emmanuel and Mansoul, all five men were sentenced to the death of the cross. Many other Diabolonians were searched out in the town, such as Mr Fooling (he was the man who had suggested handing over Captain Faith to Diabolus, you may remember), Mr Tell-Lies, Mr Mistrust, Mr Laziness, Mr Self-Love, Mr Slavish-Fear, Mr Wrong-thoughts-of-Christ and Mr No-Love. There were many in the town who were related to Mr Self-Love, so that at first his judgement was deferred; until Captain Self-Denial stood up and declared that if a rogue like Mr Self-Love were allowed to live in Mansoul, then he might as well lay down his commission at once. In fact, he and his men took the law into their own hands and executed Mr Self-Love on the spot. There were those who would have complained at this, but they dared not say anything, for when this act came to the prince's ears, he was so pleased with Captain Self-Denial that he forthwith made him a lord in Mansoul.

Chapter Eighteen

Emmanuel Speaks to His Mansoul

When Mansoul seemed at last to be in order and to enjoy peace within her gates, Emmanuel appointed a day on which he would meet all the people in the market-place, as he wished to give them a further charge concerning the future of the town. He came to the meeting place in his royal chariot, with all his captains in attendance and, after mutual greetings of love and affection, the people stood, silent and attentive, while the prince addressed them in his clear ringing voice.

"Upon you, O my Mansoul, beloved of my heart, I have bestowed many and great privileges. I have chosen you for myself and redeemed you, not only from the dread of my father's law, but out of the hand of Diabolus. This I have done, not because of your worthiness, but because I have set my heart upon you to do you good. I have bought you for myself, not with corruptible silver and gold, but at the price of my own blood, which I freely spilled to make you mine.

"I came to you first with my law and then with my gospel, to awaken you to my glory. You know well how you resisted and rebelled, yet I did not leave you, but bore patiently with your evil and stubborn ways and saved you in spite of yourselves; for am I not your long-suffering saviour? I have both reconciled you to my father and prepared mansion houses for you in his royal city. You know how many noble captains and soldiers of my father's I have lodged within your walls to be your loyal servants and to help you in the defeating of your enemies. My design in this, O my Mansoul, is to defend you, to purge, to strengthen and to sweeten you for myself, thus making you fit for my father's presence, blessing and glory. Were you not created for this purpose alone?

"You know, also, how I have healed your backslidings and forgiven you freely. When you backslid from me, I surrounded you with all manner of trials, afflicting you on every side, that you might weary of your evil ways and seek my face again. It was not *your* goodness that brought me back to you after I had, in anger, hidden myself from you. The way of backsliding was all yours, but the way of recovery was all mine. I made a hedge and a wall about you when you began to turn to things in which I do not delight; I turned your sweet to bitter, your day to night, yet at the same time confounded those who sought your destruction. It was I who set Mr Godly-Fear to work in Mansoul; it was I who stirred up Mr Conscience, Lord Understanding and Lord Willbewill after your dreadful decay. It was I who put life into you, O Mansoul, to seek me, that in finding me again you might find your health, happiness and salvation. It was I who caused the Diabolonians to withdraw from your town the second time and I who overcame them and destroyed them before your face.

"And now, my dearest Mansoul, I have returned to you in peace. Your sins against me are as if they had never been and I intend to do better for you than at your beginning. For in a little while, when a few more troubles have passed over you, I will take down your town, every stick and stone to the ground.[1] Do not be troubled when I say this, for I will carry the stones, the timber and the inhabitants to my own country, even unto the kingdom of my father. There will I raise it up again, with a strength and glory which it never had here below, so that all will admire it as a monument of my mercy for ever. And there, O Mansoul, you will have sweet and glorious fellowship with my father, with myself, and with your Lord Secretary, that you could never enjoy were you to live here below for a thousand years or more.

"There, in that land, you will never be afraid again. There will be no more threats and plots against you. You will never again hear of evil tidings, or the noise of the hideous drum of Diabolus. You will not need captains and soldiers and men of war, for there will be no more grief and sorrow, suffering or dying. In that beautiful land you will also meet many others like yourself, who have partaken of your sorrows and who expect to share your joys, whom I have redeemed and set apart for my father's court and you will all have unimaginable joy and delight in each other! Your life there will be without ending, growing ever sweeter and richer, with nothing to mar or spoil it. Besides all this, there are things which my father has prepared for those that love

[1] The prince is referring here to death.

him, which eye has never seen, nor ear heard of since the beginning of the world, treasures of his love sealed up and laid by until you are made ready to enjoy them.

"So I have told you, O Mansoul, as much as you are now able to receive, of the things reserved for you in your glorious future. In the meantime, until that day when I shall come to fetch you, listen carefully to my instructions.

"First, I charge you to keep clean and white the garments which I gave you when I first took possession of you. They are, in themselves, fine linen, but you must keep them clean and white. This will be for your honour and for my great glory. When your garments are white, all the world will know that you are mine and then shall I be delighted with your ways. Deck yourselves according to my bidding and keep to the straight and narrow path; so shall the king greatly desire your beauty, for he is your king and you shall worship him. Remember what I have told you of the fountain that I have provided, in which you may wash your garments. Go often to that fountain and never be content with unclean garments. For, as it is to my disgrace and dishonour, so it will be for your discomfort, to walk in defiled garments. My people, I have delivered you so many times from the plotting and malice of your enemies yet, for all my love and grace, I ask nothing in return, but your steadfast love and your obedient walking in my ways.

"O my Mansoul, I have lived for you, I have died for you, but I shall never die again. I live, so that you may live also. I have reconciled you to my father by the blood of my cross and, because I live, you shall live through me. I will pray for you, I will fight for you and I will yet do you good. Remember, O remember, nothing can hurt you but sin; nothing can grieve me but sin; nothing can weaken you before your enemies but sin. Therefore take heed of sin, O my Mansoul.

"Because of this, let me tell you why I still allow some Diabolonians to dwell within your walls. It is to keep you watchful and alert, to test your love for me, to cause you to prize my noble captains and soldiers and my mercy. It is so that you may never forget the deplorable condition you were once in, when you were overrun by Diabolonians and they dwelt even within Heart Castle. Listen carefully, O my Mansoul. If I were to slay all those who are now within your walls, there are yet many outside who would bring you again into bondage; for they would find you careless, perhaps sleeping, and would swallow you up in a moment. I leave them in therefore, not to do you hurt (though they will if you listen to them and serve them), but to do you good, for you must continually watch and fight against them. However they may tempt you, remember that my purpose is that they shall drive you, not further off, but *nearer* to my father, making you eager to petition him and keeping you small in your own eyes.

"Show me your love, then, O Mansoul, and let nothing take your affections from him that has redeemed you at greatest cost. Let the very sight of a Diabolonian heighten your love to your lord and prince. Stand for me, your friend, against the Diabolonians, and I will stand for you, my beloved, before my father and all his court. Love me against temptations and I will love you in spite of your infirmities.

"Learn, O my Mansoul, not to live by sense and feelings alone, but live upon my Word. Believe, when I am far from you, that yet I love you dearly and bear you upon my heart for ever. Remember that you are my beloved. As I have taught you to watch, to fight, to pray, so now I command you to believe that my love for you is constant and unchanging.

"O my Mansoul, how have I set my heart upon you, how

have I set my love upon you!

"Watch, therefore, and hold fast, until I come and take you to dwell forever in the glorious kingdom of my father."

THE HEART TAKEN

The castle of the human heart,
Strong in its native sin,
Is guarded well in every part
By him who dwells within.

For Satan there in arms resides,
And calls the place his own;
With care against assaults provides,
And rules as on a throne.

But Jesus, stronger far than he,
In his appointed hour,
Appears to set his people free
From the usurper's power.

"This heart I bought with blood," he says,
"And now it shall be mine."
His voice the strong-one armed dismays,
He knows he must resign.

In spite of unbelief and pride,
And self, and Satan's art,
The gates of brass fly open wide,
And Jesus wins the heart!

The rebel soul that once withstood
The Saviour's kindest call,
Rejoices now, by grace subdued,
To serve him with her all.

JOHN NEWTON.

APPENDIX

This appendix of selected Scriptural references is intended for those who may wish to know where to find the verses quoted, or implied, during the course of the story.

Chapter One

Page		
3	El Shaddai. Name for God translated "Almighty God".	Genesis 17: 1
	God's original creation of man in a state of innocency.	Genesis 1: 26-31
4	Satan's origin, downfall through pride and	Isaiah 14:12-15
5	banishment with the evil angels.	2 Peter 2: 4 Jude 6
	His hatred of God's purpose and people.	1 Peter 5: 8
6	Satan, in the form of a serpent (Bunyan used dragon) insinuated to Eve that God's word was not true.	Genesis 3: 1-7
8	Eve, and then Adam, succumbed to the temptation.	
9	By their one act of disobedience, Adam and Eve were immediately cut off from God, and brought under the dominion of Satan.	Genesis 3: 22-24

Chapter Two

Page		
11	Man, under the dominion of Satan, has a darkened understanding;	Ephesians 4: 17-19
12	his conscience is deadened, or hardened;	Titus 1: 15
14	his will refuses to listen to God's commands, or to walk in his ways;	Nehemiah 9: 26 Jeremiah 6: 16
	is enslaved by Satan, and fulfils the evil desires of the flesh and of the mind;	Ephesians 2: 2, 3
16	is encouraged to pursue the lusts of the flesh, the lusts of the eyes and the pride of life.	1 John 2: 15-16

Chapter Three

Page		
19	Reference to the plans of the Godhead, before the foundation of the world, to restore mankind from its state of sin and misery.	Ephesians 1: 4 Romans 9: 22, 23 Acts 15: 18
	The grief of God over the sin of mankind.	Genesis 6: 5-6
20	Emmanuel means "God with us".	Matthew 1: 22-23
	God the Son's intention to enter the world and make a once-and-for-all atonement for the sin of mankind.	Hebrews 2: 14, 15 Hebrews 7: 26, 27
	This plan to be made known to men through the revelation of the Holy Scriptures.	Hebrews 1: 1-2
21	The angels brought this message to the world, before the record of Scripture was complete.	Luke 2: 9-14
22	Satan endeavours to bind man in a covenant of evil with himself, hoping that even God will not be able to set him free from it.	Isaiah 28: 15
24	The provision of the diabolical armour (compared with the armour of light provided for the Christian in Ephesians 6: 10-17):	
	(a) "vain-hope" that all will be well in the end	Deuteronomy 29: 19
	(b) "a hard heart" (breastplate of iron)	Revelation 9: 9 Zechariah 7: 12
25	(c) "an evil tongue" (sword)	Psalm 57: 4 Psalm 64: 2-3 James 3: 6-8
	(d) "unbelief" (shield)	Matthew 13: 58
	(e) "a prayerless spirit"	Job 21: 15

CHAPTER FOUR

Page		
27	God first sends his law to bring men to obedience	Galatians 3: 24 Deuteronomy 29: 29 John 1: 17
	he commands all men to repent.	Acts 17: 30
28	Captain Boanerges (the meaning of this name).	Mark 3: 17
	Captain Conviction (the book of the law).	Deuteronomy 31: 26
	Captain Judgement (the fiery furnace).	Matthew 13: 40–42
	Captain Execution (the axe at the root of the tree).	Matthew 3: 10
29	First, an offer of peace.	Luke 10: 5
30	"Help! Help! The men that turn the world upside down."	Acts 17: 6
31	"Take-heed-what-you-hear."	Mark 4: 24
	The need to compel men to hear.	Luke 14: 23
34	None can stand against the anger of God.	Psalm 2: 11–12 Ezekiel 22: 14
35	God does not desire the death of the sinner.	Ezekiel 33: 11 2 Peter 3: 9
	The day of the Lord, the day of judgement, will come.	Joel 2: 11 Malachi 4: 1 2 Peter 3: 10
	He has prepared his throne for judgement.	Psalm 9: 7
36	The parable of the barren fig-tree.	Luke 13: 6–9
	The sinner's determination not to listen.	Zechariah 7: 11, 12

CHAPTER FIVE

Page		
39	"Ye must be born again."	John 3: 3–7
40	Attacks by Satan	Ephesians 6: 12

CHAPTER SIX

Page		
48	The heavens and stars the works of God's fingers.	Psalm 8: 3-4
50	The sinner makes light of God's offers of mercy.	Proverbs 1: 23-25
51	Emmanuel, God the Son, delights to do his Father's will.	Psalm 40: 8 Hebrews 10: 7
	He is the captain of our salvation.	Hebrews 2: 10
52	Captain Faith (the holy lamb and the shield).	John 1: 29 Ephesians 6: 16
	Captain Good-Hope (the three golden anchors).	Hebrews 6: 19
	Captain Love (a loving embrace).	1 Corinthians 13
	Captain Purity (three golden doves).	Luke 3: 22
	Captain Patience (three golden arrows piercing the heart).	Hebrews 6: 12
56	Emmanuel, God's Son, is the heir of all things and the Father's delight is in him.	Hebrews 1: 2 Isaiah 42: 1 Matthew 12: 18 Proverbs 8: 30
	All things have been given into his hand by the Father.	John 3: 35
	Heaven and earth will pass away, but God's Word cannot be broken.	Matthew 5: 18
57	God's Son desires to save, not to destroy.	Luke 9: 56
	He is stronger than "the strong man armed".	Luke 11: 21-22
	He is mighty to save.	Isaiah 63: 1
	The deliberate blocking of the ears against God's Word.	Zechariah 7: 11

CHAPTER SEVEN

Page		
59	The deceit of the heart being willing to submit only a part to God.	Acts 5: 1-5
	Emmanuel will lose none of those who have been given him.	John 6: 39 John 17: 6-12

60	The Christian must seek to cleanse his life of every trace of the old life of sin.	1 Corinthians 5: 7–8 Galatians 5: 24 Colossians 3: 5–9 Romans 6: 12–13
	All problems, of all kinds, are to be brought to God in prayer.	Philippians 4: 6
61	Emmanuel's Word is as a two-edged sword.	Hebrews 4: 12
62	The devil will disguise himself as an "angel of light" to achieve his ends.	2 Corinthians 11: 14
	By the works of the flesh shall no man be justified.	Galatians 2: 16
63	The malice of Satan when he sees that he is to be cast out of a soul.	Mark 9: 26–27
67	The Lord Jesus Christ spoils principalities and powers, and leads captivity captive.	Colossians 2: 15 Ephesians 4: 8

CHAPTER EIGHT

Page		
76	". . . beauty for ashes, the oil of joy for mourning. . . ."	Isaiah 61: 1–3
	The everlasting arms of God.	Deuteronomy 33: 27
	"Blessed be the glory of the Lord from this place. . . ."	Ezekiel 3: 12

CHAPTER NINE

Page		
79	Good tidings of great joy.	Luke 2: 10
80	The bountiful dealings of the Lord.	Psalm 116: 7–8
	He does not deal with us as we deserve.	Psalm 103: 10
	"The Lord, the Lord God, merciful and gracious. . . ."	Exodus 34: 6
83	The Lord Jesus Christ takes up residence in the renewed heart.	Ephesians 3: 17

	Feeding upon the Word of God, especially his promises.	Jeremiah 15: 16 1 Peter 2: 2
	The water that was turned into wine.	John 2: 1-11

CHAPTER TEN

Page		
93	The crucifying of the lusts of the flesh.	Romans 6: 12-14 Galatians 5: 24

CHAPTER ELEVEN

Page		
95	"The dead lion and the dead bear (reference to David's experience, although only a young man).	1 Samuel 17: 36-37
	"Old things are passed away, behold, all things are become new. . . ."	2 Corinthians 5: 17
96	All sins and iniquities are forgiven by the Lord.	Hebrews 8: 12
	The law and testament and all things therein, for everlasting comfort and joy.	Hebrews 7: 22 Hebrews 8: 6
	The grace of the Father and Son to be in the believer's heart.	Colossians 3: 16 1 John 4: 16
	The benefit of all things, present and yet to come.	1 Corinthians 3: 21-22
	Unhindered access to the Father at all times.	Hebrews 10: 19-20 Matthew 7: 7
	These blessings only for believers.	2 Corinthians 6: 14-16
	The new covenant made with the believer.	Jeremiah 31: 33-34 Hebrews 8: 10-12
97	Teachers and guides are necessary if believers are to know and do the Father's will.	Ephesians 4: 11-13 1 Corinthians 12:28

	The teaching and ministry of the Holy Spirit.	1 Thessalonians 1: 5–6 1 John 2: 20, 27
	He is not to be grieved.	Ephesians 4: 30
98	He brings forgotten things back to remembrance.	John 14: 26
	He must guide in all prayers made to the Father.	Jude 20 Ephesians 6: 18 Romans 8: 26
	If he is grieved, he may turn and become an enemy.	Isaiah 63: 10
	He alone can shed abroad the love of God in the heart.	Romans 5: 5
	"He that hath an ear to hear, let him hear what the Spirit saith unto the churches. . . ."	Revelation 2: 7, 11, 17, 29
	Evil desires still lie hidden within the old nature.	Romans 6: 12
99	The believer is arrayed in the fine white linen of the saints (the robe of Christ's righteousness).	Revelation 19: 8 Isaiah 61: 10
	These garments to be kept always clean and white.	Revelation 3: 4
100	God delights to walk and dwell among his people.	2 Corinthians 6: 16
101	The Lord Jesus Christ knocks at the door of the heart (and of his church) seeking to come in and have fellowship with his people.	Revelation 3: 20 Song of Solomon 5: 2
	God's peace resides in the renewed heart, and is closely related to faith and hope.	Colossians 3: 15 Romans 15: 13

Chapter Twelve

Page		
106	The danger of being lulled into heedlessness and carelessness.	Deuteronomy 8: 11–20
	"Oh that my people had hearkened unto me. . . ."	Psalm 81: 13–16 Isaiah 48: 18
107	"Have I been such a wilderness. . . ."	Jeremiah 2: 31–32

	The danger of walking in evil ways.	Leviticus 26: 23–24
	Grieving the Holy Spirit.	Ephesians 4: 30 1 Thessalonians 5: 19
108	"I will return to my place until they acknowledge their offence. . . ."	Hosea 5: 15
	God's peace departs from the back-sliding heart.	Ezekiel 11: 21
110	The disturbed conscience seeks the Lord – in vain.	Song of Solomon 5: 6
	The Holy Spirit remains in the heart, but withholds his help.	Isaiah 63: 10
111	Subject of the sermon.	Jonah 2: 8
	Feeble knees, lame feet, things ready to die.	Hebrews 12: 12 Revelation 3: 2
	White garments soiled and bedraggled.	Jude 23
112	The barren fig-tree.	Luke 13: 6–9
	Heaven shut to prayer.	Lamentations 3: 8, 44
	The backslider accused of deserting the Lord in time of prosperity, and only calling upon him in trouble.	Zechariah 7: 13 Jeremiah 2: 27–28

CHAPTER THIRTEEN

Page		
116	The rage and hatred of Satan, as a roaring lion.	1 Peter 5: 8
118	The Lord will not regard prayers, while iniquity is entertained in the heart.	Psalm 66: 18 Isaiah 59: 1–2
	The need to rend the heart, and not the garments, a sign of real prayer and repentance.	Joel 2: 12–15

CHAPTER FOURTEEN

Page		
121	Determination to guard diligently against Satan's attack.	1 Corinthians 16: 13

	Heart-searching encouraged – to find any root of evil.	Lamentations 3: 40 Hebrews 12: 15–16
	A fast and a solemn assembly called for.	Joel 1: 14
122	Satan, resisted, is compelled to withdraw.	James 4: 7
123	"Your back-slidings shall reprove you. . . ."	Jeremiah 2: 19
124	The well-aimed sling-stones.	Zechariah 9: 15

CHAPTER FIFTEEN

Page		
127	Although in a back-slidden condition, the believer knows that he was turned from darkness to light, and from the power of Satan to God.	1 Peter 2: 9 Colossians 1: 13
129	Satan can cause great darkness and misery in the heart of the backslider, even though he cannot get into the heart.	Isaiah 5: 29–30
131	A petition for deliverance.	Jeremiah 14: 7–9 Psalm 25: 16–19
132	The back-slider filled with shame and confusion.	Daniel 9: 4–10
	"Established, strengthened and settled."	1 Peter 5: 10
133	The reproach of the enemy "Where is your God?"	Psalm 42: 10
	"Him that cometh unto me I will in no wise cast out."	John 6: 37
	"Rejoice not against me, O mine enemy. . . ."	Micah 7: 8
135	"Without faith it is impossible to please God. . . ."	Hebrews 11: 6

CHAPTER SIXTEEN

Page		
139	The snare of Laodicea.	Revelation 3: 14–17
	The deceitfulness of riches chokes the Word.	Matthew 13: 22

	Drunkenness and the cares of this life do the same.	Luke 21: 34
140	The Holy Spirit alone can interpret the will of God.	1 Corinthians 2: 11
141	The Word of God is as a two-edged sword.	Hebrews 4: 12
143	"Peace be unto you. . . ."	John 20: 19
	"Lift up your heads, O ye gates. . . ."	Psalm 24: 7-10
144	"Blessed is he that cometh in the name of the Lord. . . ."	Matthew 21: 1-11
	". . . for the joy of the Lord is your strength. . . ."	Nehemiah 8: 10
	The lamenting, and genuine sorrow, for past sin and the kisses of pardon.	Luke 15: 20-21
	The fountain opened for sin and uncleanness.	Zechariah 13: 1
145	The return of God's peace.	Philippians 4: 7

CHAPTER SEVENTEEN

Page		
147	Captain Cain (the murdering bands).	Genesis 4: 8
	Captain Ishmael (the mocking bands).	Genesis 21: 9-10
	Captain Esau (grudging a blessing).	Genesis 27: 41-45
	Captain Saul (jealous and furious).	1 Samuel 18: 6-11; 19: 8-11
	Captain Absalom (killer of father or friend).	2 Samuel 15: 13-14
	Captain Judas (betrayer of a friend for money).	Matthew 26: 14-16
	The Blood-thirsty men.	Isaiah 59: 7 Psalm 26: 9-10 Jeremiah 22: 17
148	"Lord, save us from these blood-thirsty men. . . ."	Psalm 59: 2
150	Some oppose the Lord out of sheer ignorance, they repent and they receive mercy.	1 Timothy 1: 13 Luke 23: 34

Page		
	They also tremble with fear.	Acts 9: 5-6
	The unrepentant are bound over until the day of judgement.	2 Peter 2: 9

CHAPTER EIGHTEEN

Page		
155	Our redemption was purchased, not with silver and gold, but with the precious blood of Christ.	1 Peter 1: 18-19
	The healing of back-sliding.	Jeremiah 3: 14, 22 Hosea 14: 4
156	Our transgressions are as if they had never been.	Isaiah 44: 22
	In heaven there will be no more sorrow, suffering, trials or death.	Revelation 21: 4
157	There are blessings laid up in heaven that eye has never seen, nor ear heard.	1 Corinthians 2: 9 Isaiah 64: 4
	"He is thy Lord and worship thou him. . . ."	Psalm 45: 11
	Warning against having filthy garments.	Zechariah 3: 3-4
	Continual cleansing needed.	Zechariah 13: 1
158	The need to live continually upon God's Word, and to walk by faith, not feelings.	Deuteronomy 8: 3 Job 23: 12 2 Corinthians 5: 7